# Caught Between My Husband and a Hustler

K.L. HALL

K.L. HALL PRODUCTIONS

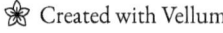 Created with Vellum

# Synopsis

For five years, Hermès Capone thought she had the perfect love story. As a trophy wife and mother of two beautiful daughters, she spent her time tucked away in the elite suburbs of Philadelphia, living the fairytale she'd always dreamed of. Her only complaint was that her love life lacked the thrill that it once used to. As beautiful as she may be, she remains forgotten in her husband's eyes.

Julius "Cap" Capone is the best criminal defense attorney money can buy. He specializes in helping criminals with dirty money and even dirtier criminal backgrounds. He's just taken on Philly's biggest hustler, Nario "Rio" Sullivan, as his new client in hopes of getting his charges dropped and an even bigger payout. When Rio and Hermès meet for the first time, she immediately feels a carnal attraction to him. Could it be his dark chocolate eyes, perfect smile, or muscular build? Whatever the case, her eyes aren't the only part of her body that wants more of him.

When rumors of her husband's infidelity arise, she has to decide if she will withstand the storm that is threatening to tear down her entire household or taste the forbidden fruit that is Rio Sullivan. Between the lust and the lies, everyone knows love is not picture-perfect. All parties are playing with a fire so hot that everyone is sure to get burned. Will

Hermès succumb to her broken heart to save face and status or give in to the attraction that won't fade between her and Rio? Only one man can have what's left of her heart.

# Epigraph

*"You've got to learn to leave the table when love's no longer being served."*
*-Nina Simone*

## CHAPTER 1

# Lucky Number Six

## Hermès Capone

I listened to my Christian Louboutin heels click *left, right, left, right* as I made my way across the marble flooring in the lobby of the Ritz Carlton in the heart of Philadelphia.

"Good afternoon. I'd like to check into my room. Reservations should be under my husband's name, Mr. Julius Capone," I told the hotel attendant as I sat my five-thousand-dollar handbag on the counter.

"Ah, yes, Mrs. Capone. Here is your key. You are in suite twenty-five-forty-eight," he told me.

"Thank you." I smiled.

I took the elevator to the twenty-fifth floor, entered the room, and looked around. My eyes immediately locked on the box of chocolates on top of the crimson rose petals scattered across the California king-sized bed and the bouquet in a vase beside the TV. *He's stepping it up this year.*

Six years ago, Julius Alexander Capone and I had chosen to consummate our love and became husband and wife at the age of twenty-five. He'd just passed the bar exam and landed a job as a junior attorney at one of Philadelphia's largest law firms. I couldn't have been prouder of *my* man. Just one month after we said, 'I Do,' I said, 'I'm pregnant,' and nine months later, we welcomed our first daughter, Symphony, into the world. Two years later, Symphony was joined by her younger sister, Melody.

I couldn't have been more excited for us to spend some much-needed quality time together to work on baby number three, our son. It'd been so long since we'd spent time between just the two of us due to the demands of his high-paying and high-stress job. Cap was one of his firm's top criminal defense attorneys and played a massive role in getting all the big-time criminals out of doing lengthy sentences. Although I admired my husband for his dedication to his job, my body had been longing to make love to him all over the room, which cost well over six hundred dollars a night.

I put my purse down, walked over to the bed, and picked up the box of chocolates. A note attached read, *"Meet me for dinner downstairs at seven. Love, Cap."* I smiled and kicked off my heels, then headed to the bathroom. The heated floors felt like heaven against the soles of my feet as I went to the soaking tub to run myself a nice long bath. I was going to enjoy the serenity of the remainder of the day and rest up so I could be an animal for my husband all night long.

While the bathtub filled with warm, soapy water, I cracked open the box of chocolates and popped one into my mouth. I chewed slowly as my eyes rolled back in my head. He'd gotten my favorite, Godiva. I turned on some smooth jams as I stepped out of the bathroom to pour myself a glass of wine from the small bottle inside the minibar. Then, I got undressed and spent the next hour and a half soaking in the tub until my skin was pruned and the water was cold, all because I'd gotten caught up fantasizing about Cap.

I pulled myself out of the tub and slid one of the luxurious bathrobes over my body while stuffing my toes into the matching slippers. My head rested against the cottony soft pillows as my hand fell in between my thighs. It took everything in me not to play with my flower. I'd been so horny over the past few weeks. It was almost as if every time I saw something that even resembled a penis, I wanted to fuck it.

"Yeah, Cap is about to get this work tonight," I mumbled.

* * *

By the time I opened my eyes and looked at the clock, it was already five minutes past six. I quickly shot up out of the bed and started doing my hair and makeup. When I was done, I slid on a skin-tight black dress that stopped right above my knee, some strappy black heels, and sprayed a few squirts of Cap's favorite perfume on my wrists, behind my ears, and on my neck so I was sure he'd smell it from across the room. Before walking out of the suite, I gave myself another once-over. As good as I looked, we probably wouldn't make it through the first course.

While walking towards the restaurant downstairs, I passed by elite couples' arm in arm or holding hands and showing public affection towards one another, which made me smile. The smell of gourmet dining wafted past my nose as I entered the lobby restaurant. There were people everywhere. I glanced down at my phone and clicked the side. It was seven minutes past seven. *Perfect.* I smiled to myself.

"Good evening, ma'am. Do you have reservations?" the hostess asked me.

"Um, yes. My husband and I have reservations for seven p.m. under Julius Capone," I responded.

"Capone...Capone..." she scrolled with her finger.

"Is there something wrong?"

"Um, I'm not quite sure. We had a reservation for a Julius Capone here earlier at six o'clock, but I don't see anything for seven."

"There must be some mistake. He told me we had dinner reservations here at seven o'clock sharp. Can you please just check again?" I asked, feeling flustered.

I quickly glanced behind me and saw that a line had formed, which made me even more antsy. I shifted my weight from one leg to the other while I watched her scroll her manicured fingernail down the tablet again.

"Nothing?" I asked.

"No, ma'am, I'm sorry. I could try to get you in if another couple drops out, but we're booked solid through the end of the night right now."

I swallowed the lump in my throat and shook my head. "No, thank you. That um...that won't be necessary. I'm going to step aside and call my husband to figure all of this out. Excuse me."

I could feel my face turning red as I turned and faced all of the couples behind me. I quickly jetted out of the restaurant and stepped off to a secluded corner to call Cap. His phone rang six times and then went to voicemail. *"You've reached Julius Capone, attorney at law. I can't get to my phone right now. Please leave a message at..."*

*'CLICK'*

As flustered as I was, I was more hurt than anything. Cap was a strategic man. He would never mix up reservations unless his paralegal Tia did it. She was a young paralegal who worked under his supervision and some-times doubled as his executive assistant. I could tell she had eyes for him. Anytime I went to his office and saw her interactions with him, it was almost like she was undressing him with her little beady ass eyes. Steam puffed out of my nose as I redialed his number. The same thing happened, so I texted him.

*Me: 7:22 p.m.: Baby, I'm at the restaurant, and there's been some sort of mistake with our reservations. Where are you? Call me back!*

I saw the three ellipses that told me he was responding, but then they disappeared. *What the fuck,* I growled to myself. I called him back one more time, and he didn't answer. It didn't even ring. His phone had gone straight to voicemail. *Maybe he's in a bad reception area, lost service, or is trying to call me back.*

I paced the marble floor back and forth, calling and calling until my feet began to hurt. I walked towards the other side of the lobby and headed to the bar to sit down. Although there were still quite a few people in there, there weren't as many as inside the restaurant. I plopped down in the high bar seat and put my phone on the counter.

"What can I get you?" the bartender asked.

"Um, a glass of champagne," I told him.

"Coming right up."

* * *

Two glasses of champagne and twenty phone calls later, I was still sitting alone. At a bar. On my fucking anniversary. Cap had done some fucked up things in the past, but nothing like that. I let out the loudest sigh my body could muster as I looked around the room. Fresh white tablecloths were on all the tables, and red rose petals and lit candles were used as centerpieces. My eyes rolled just as my stomach growled.

"Can I please see a menu?" I asked.

The bartender handed me a menu; nothing made my mouth water. I sighed and put the menu down beside me.

"Another glass of champagne while you wait?"

"Yeah, sure. Why the hell not," I huffed.

An hour and a half later, my battery was on ten percent, and my patience was on zero. I swiped my key, returned to my room, and looked around, getting mad all over again. It was the first time in hours that I realized I *still* hadn't heard back from Cap. I stormed over to the bed and swatted the rose petals onto the floor.

"Stupid mothafucka!" I growled as I threw my heels across the room.

I huffed in anger as they clanged against the wall, then flung my body across the bed.

## CHAPTER 2

# Hiroshima

**Hermès**

Cap and I hadn't spoken outside of an 'I'm sorry' and a 'fuck you' since my letdown on our anniversary. It had been a week, and I was still livid. The wound was still fresh in my book and would continue. There was no excuse good enough for my ears.

"Have a good day, girls. Mommy loves you," I said, snapping out of my daze as I pulled up to the girls' school and dropped them off.

"Love you, too," my five-year-old daughter, Symphony, told me.

The school attendant closed my door for me as I rolled down the window to watch them get inside the school safely before pulling off.

"Have a good day, Mrs. Capone," the man told me.

I nodded. "Thanks. You, too."

Before returning home, I swung by Starbucks to get my usual: a Grande, iced, sugar-free, vanilla latte with soy milk. I was a complicated Starbucks regular, so they didn't even question my obnoxious order anymore. I wrapped my lips around the green straw and headed back home.

As soon as I pulled into my driveway, I saw a white Mercedes parked in front of the house that I didn't recognize. Instead of pulling up behind it and getting out, I pulled up beside it and rolled down the window to see Tia, Cap's paralegal, sitting inside.

"Can I help you?" I asked after blowing my horn, so she'd notice me.

"Hermès..."

"Tia? What are you doing here? Cap isn't—"

"I know he's not here. That's why I came, to talk to you woman to woman."

My brows snapped together. "About what?"

"Can we talk?"

My forehead creased, and I slowly nodded before putting the truck in park and getting out. I first noticed her tear-stained eyes when she closed the car door and looked at me. The next was her protruding pregnant belly.

"Tia, what could we possibly need to talk about?" I asked, scrunching up my forehead as if I smelled something foul.

She looked down at her stomach and then back up at me. "It's his, Hermès."

I raised my arched eyebrow at her. "His who?"

"I'm carrying Cap's baby."

My eyes widened as I slowly licked my lips. All I could do was shake my head in disbelief. My brain was yelling out a million commands to the rest of my body. *Punch the bitch. Cuss her ass out.* Yet, my body was frozen as if someone had pressed pause on my entire life. Cap wouldn't do me like that. Not me. Not his *wife*.

"There must be some mistake." I managed to mumble out.

"Look, I know this is a lot for you to swallow, and by the look on your face, I can tell this is your first time hearing about this baby or me, isn't it?"

My lips parted to respond as I crossed my arms over my chest. "Yeah, and that's exactly why I'm calling bullshit on all of this. Cap and I talk every night, and he's never mentioned you being pregnant. Not even *once*."

"Obviously, he doesn't tell you everything. He's been telling me for months that he was going to tell you, and I—"

I gave a dismissive wave, and she quickly closed her flapping lips. "What is it that you want, Tia? Huh? Is it money? Are you tired of working for a check, and now you just wanna lay up somewhere and get paid? Is that it?"

She sucked her teeth. "Look, all I want is for Cap to do right by *our* son and me."

Her words crushed my spirit. I was supposed to have been the only woman with Cap's children. The four of us were a unit, and now there was a bitch standing in my face telling me that she was carrying another sibling for my children that came from my husband's sperm. I was on fire. My eyes cut through her with disgust. She looked to be in her very early twenties. Even with the pregnant belly, I could tell she didn't weigh much. Her skin was sandalwood brown, and she had decent facial features. Her face may have looked grown, but her eyes said she was a scared ass little girl.

"Get the fuck off my property, bitch."

"Look, he fired me yesterday, and I just want to know if you were behind it! This is discrimination! I will go to the board, and he will lose his license for this!"

"You think I give a fuck about you losin' your job? Why would you even come to me on this shit and then threaten my husband in the same breath?"

She huffed. "Look, I—"

"How long?" I asked, throwing up my hand and waving her words away.

"How long what?"

I shot her a hateful look. "How long have you been fucking my husband, you dim-witted bitch?"

She tucked her lips and then slowly opened her mouth to speak. "The affair started a few months after I started working there, and now I guess it's over because he fired me yesterday. I came here because he told me that you were behind it."

"Me? Why the fuck would I be behind it? I thought your job was to file fucking papers, not fuck other people's husbands!"

"He told me that when he told you about me and the baby, you wanted me gone."

I scoffed, followed by a quick chuckle. "And you believed that? Sounds like to me he got tired of your fast ass."

"I love him..." her voice shook.

"You love him? Guess what? I love him, too! You know who else loves him? OUR KIDS! MY KIDS! You can't have my life!"

"He loves me too, Hermès. I'm sorry, but we're going to be together. The quicker you can accept that, the better it'll be for all of us. I want Jr. to have a good relationship with his older sisters."

My eyes damn near bugged out of my head. If I wasn't too pretty for jail, I would've wrapped my hands around her lanky ass throat and never let go.

Instead, I scoffed. "I can't believe you had the audacity to stand here in my face and say that shit to me. You should be on your knees begging that I don't call the police on your ass for trespassing on my property! You don't even have the common sense to apologize to me! His wife! Let me give you a word of mothafuckin advice, Tia. Cap don't love you. He loves what you do for him. And now, he probably don't even want that. So, I suggest you get back in that raggedy ass Benz you got in my driveway and drive the fuck off and never, ever bring your ass back to my house again!"

She turned to get back inside her car, and I stood on the side and watched her pull off. A part of me didn't know why I had even wasted that much of my breath on her, but somebody needed to let her ass know that life didn't hand out too many fairytales, and there was no way I was going to let her have even a piece of mine. Instead of going inside the house and calming down like a woman in her right mind would've, I hopped back inside my Rolls Royce truck and headed straight to Cap's office. That bitch Tia clearly wanted the smoke over my husband, and I was going to bring hell right to his front door.

* * *

I illegally parked my truck in front of the high-rise building where Cap worked downtown and shut off the engine. My feet thudded against the cold, paved steps as I marched into the building and headed for the elevator. When the elevator dinged, I stepped out with a mug on my face that made people look the other way.

"I need to speak to Julius Capone," I said, interrupting the receptionist's phone call.

She sliced her eyes up at me and frowned for a split second. "One moment, ma'am."

"I don't have a moment; I need to speak with him now!" I said, raising my voice an octave higher.

She quickly looked at the calendar pulled up on one of her computer screens and looked back at me. "He's with a client right now," she whispered with her hand over the phone receiver.

I could hear other phone lines ringing in the distance as I tapped my foot against the polished hardwood floor. I rubbed my temples, trying to calm down, but to no avail. My nerves tinged like a timer on an oven, and I lost it. "I don't give a fuck if he's with the good Lord himself! I need to speak to my husband right now!"

I brushed past her desk and walked straight into his office. The door flung open so fast it ricocheted against the wall, slamming against the Penn State alum plaque on the wall next to his law degrees. His entire office smelled of his favorite cologne. It was my favorite, too. I'd bought it for him as a surprise when we went to Paris in the summer past.

"Hermès?"

My knees buckled when my eyes landed on him, and my heart beat faster.

"Baby, what are you doing here?" he asked, pushing himself out of his rolling desk chair while straightening his tie.

I took a deep, silent breath before speaking. "Cap, I need to speak with you *now*."

His dark brown eyes widened, then went back to normal size. "I'm with a client right now. Can it wait until later when I get home?"

"No, Cap. It can't. It's...*very* important."

"Are the girls okay?" he asked.

I shook my head as my eyes landed on the framed photos of us on our wedding day and the latest family photo we'd taken on his desk. *What a fuckin' joke*, I thought to myself. He didn't give a fuck about those pictures when he probably had that stupid bitch bent over his desk while I was at home raising our children. It was clear to me that he didn't give a fuck about us, only himself.

"Are they?" he asked with urgency in his voice.

"They're fine, Cap."

He massaged the back of his neck as if he was more stressed out than I was. "Okay, so can we please talk about whatever you want to talk about at home?"

I squeezed my eyes shut as my nostrils flared. Instead of responding with words, I walked over to his desk and pushed the stack of files onto the floor along with his gold-plated nameplate.

"Now!" I yelled.

When the words fell off my lips, his client turned around and locked eyes with me. The first thing I noticed was his dark chocolate eyes. And for a second, I was stupefied by his presence. He had beautiful white teeth and a set of beautiful cherry-colored lips. Even though he was sitting down, I could easily tell he had a broad chest and strong muscles. Perhaps the sexiest thing of all was the beard that wrapped around the lower half of his chocolate-colored face.

"I can step out for a second," he spoke up, looking dead at me.

Cap and I both spoke up in unison. "Yeah, that would be best," I bellowed.

"No, you don't have to do that," Cap objected.

I went poker-faced as heat stained my cheeks. He was not ready for the storm I was about to rain down on him. "Fine, you wanna do this shit right here and now? You got it."

I went dead silent for about fifteen painfully long seconds. I knew I was taking a risk by asking him the questions at his job and during a meeting with another one of his hoodlum-ass clients, but I didn't care. Every atom in my body needed to know the truth.

"Your paralegal whore stopped by the house to see me this morning."

The color instantly drained from his face. I could see the frustration on his face without me having even mentioned her name. He knew exactly what the can of worms I'd opened were about to taste like. I'd just lit the fuse that would blow up his entire life.

"She says it's your baby. Is it true?"

His jaws clenched together like three-ton walls closing in on each other. I could tell he

was madder that his bitch had ratted him out than he was over being caught up in the first place.

"Can we please talk about this later?" he asked through his white, clenched teeth.

My lower lip trembled. "Do you love her, Julius?"

His mouth set in a hard line. "What? Hermès, stop."

My lips drew back in a snarl. "Answer the fuckin' question. Do you love her?" I asked again.

The sadness in my eyes tore into his. He'd hurt me, and he needed to know what hurting his wife looked like. My heart was bleeding right in front of him and a stranger that I didn't even know.

"I—"

"Whatever comes out of your mouth next better be the truth," I warned him.

His face went blank before he let out a long breath. "I—I don't know."

My eyes widened. I expected him to curse, defend his manhood, and not embarrass himself or me. But he'd done the exact opposite. He'd crushed the last beating piece of my heart.

Without saying another word, I spun around on my heels. Tears shimmered in my eyes, but I refused to let them fall. He wouldn't have the luxury of seeing me wash away into a puddle of tears. Neither he nor his client.

"Baby, wait," Cap called out before my hand hit the door.

I jerked my neck back in his direction with fire in my eyes. "Get back to work, Cap. You're going to need as much money as you can when I'm through with your ass."

## CHAPTER 3

# *The Tell-Tale Heart*

**Hermès**

Hours later, my nerves were still prickling, as if I'd been getting stuck with tiny cacti. There was so much rage bottled up inside of me. Anxiety swirled around me as if I was stuck on a merry-go-round. I'd been drowning my sorrows in a bottle of wine since I'd gotten the girls from school. My ears perked up the second I heard Cap's keys jingle inside the lock. It was late. The girls were fast asleep. It was about to be round two.

The second my eyes landed on his, I spoke without giving him a chance to take off his shoes. "How far along is she? Tell me the truth."

He removed his coat silently and slid off his designer dress shoes by the door. I knew he was intentionally drawing things out. If the silence between us continued, I didn't know if I would survive.

"Six months," he said, looking past me.

All the air left my lungs, and my chest caved in as if I'd been hit with a sack of rocks.

"How many times did you fuck her?"

"I don't know."

My mind was all over the place. There were so many questions I wanted to ask that they were all fighting to escape past my lips without allowing my brain to organize them.

"Would you fuck that bitch and then come home to fuck me? Are you that fuckin' triflin', nigga?"

"I don't know," he replied again.

"Wow...wow! Wow! And you stand here in my face and tell me that you don't know if you fucked her then fucked me? Are you that fucked up in the fuckin' head, Cap? Do you fuckin' love the bitch? And don't you dare tell me you don't fuckin' know!" I yelled.

He lifted his chin, and I saw a vein popping out of his neck. "I don't want to talk about this anymore, Hermès."

"That's too damn bad! Look at this!" I said, swiping a piece of paper off the dining room table and holding it out for him to grab.

"What is it?"

"Read it."

"I don't want to read shit right now, Hermès."

"Read the fucking paper, Cap!"

He snatched it from my hand and let his eyes read across the creased sheet of pink construction paper from left to right. "What is this?"

"Symphony made it in class today."

His harsh brow softened, and he let his brain take in the words his eyes were reading. "When I grow up, I want to be married like my mommy and daddy," he mumbled.

I scoffed. "Now, what am I going to say to her when she asks me why mommy and daddy don't look like the kissing stick figures on that piece of fuckin' paper, huh?"

"What do you want me to do with this? Huh? You think I fuckin' wanted shit to be this way? I wanted to tell you for a long time, but whenever I was around you or the girls...I just knew it would hurt you too much."

"And even then, the possibility of our pain didn't stop you from stickin' your dick in another bitch."

"None of it matters now because it's over!" he yelled.

"What do you mean none of it matters? Everything matters to me, Cap! This isn't just my life that you're fucking with! What did she give you that I never did? A threesome? A son? Huh? I thought we were both in agreeance that we were going to work on our third baby. Is this why you don't touch me? Because you got another bitch pregnant?"

"At first, it was a mistake..."

"A mistake that you kept on making, right? Tell me this, Cap. Why her?" I paused. "I get my nails and hair done on the regular and keep my body right after two kids, nigga! Two! I weigh the same amount as I did when we first met! And you got the nerve to stand here in my face and tell me that you want somebody else?"

"I don't know what I want."

"It's clear you don't want me or your daughters!"

"Listen, I'm going out of town on business for the weekend. Maybe I'll be ready to talk about it when I come back. I just need some time to get my head together, all right? But I promise you, we will talk."

"You might be returning to an empty house when you do," I warned him.

Cap quickly stepped into my shadow, hovering over me. "There will never come a time where it's okay for you to think that you can take my kids away from me."

"Don't act like you give a fuck about them now when you didn't give a fuck about what your actions would do to them when you were sticking your dick where it didn't belong!"

"I'm not fuckin' playin' with you, Hermès! You and my daughters will be here when I get back."

I rolled my eyes. My emotions were on a rollercoaster. I'd gone from frantic to enraged and then uncontrollable sadness. The tears I'd dared to let him see had sprung out of my eyes like water in a sprinkler. I could feel my heart pumping at a pace I knew was hazardous to me and everyone around me. I wiped my tears, smearing my mascara across my face.

"What the fuck have I ever done but love you, Cap? Huh? I gave you two beautiful children and all of me, and you just... do me like this? Huh? How could you do this to me? I'm your wife! Do you want to get a divorce? Is that what you want?" I asked.

A divorce meant leaving. Leaving meant starting over alone with two children. A part of me seemed to be torn between what I knew I deserved and the life I had gotten comfortable living. I would be a fool if I said I didn't still love him, but I was tired of always being the one putting out fires and the only one getting fuckin' burnt. I hated Julius for what he'd done to me, to us. But that was the thing about love...it made you do stupid shit.

"I told you I don't want to talk about this shit anymore! I just need time to clear my head and think all this through," he told me as he pulled his keys out of his pocket.

"So that's it? You're just going to turn your back on me? Your bitch don't owe me nothin', Cap, but you owe me and your daughters every fuckin' thing," I said to his back.

"I gotta go," he said, closing the door behind him.

\* \* \*

### Julius 'Cap' Capone

I knew she would never forgive me the second I walked through that door. I wouldn't forgive me if I were in her shoes. I'd done some foul shit to her over the years, but she never flinched. She never folded. Seeing her fall like a house of cards hurt, mainly because it was my fault. I tossed my body into the driver's seat of my Lexus and pressed the button to start the engine.

I looked back and saw Hermès standing at the front door, waiting for me to leave. I pulled off, not caring if I had to buy a new wardrobe while I was out of town for the weekend. I was not going back into that house until she calmed down. Deep down, I knew I was fucked. I had both an angry wife and an angry side chick. If I couldn't control the way Hermès was feeling, at least I knew I still had Tia wrapped around my dick.

Instead of hitting the interstate to head North to New York, I decided to pop up at Tia's apartment and get her in check before I left. Before I shut the engine off, my phone lit up to a picture of Hermès, the girls, and me as my screensaver. I quickly locked my phone and sighed.

Tia opened the door for me with a smug look on her face. "Didn't expect to see you back over here for a while. What she do? Throw your ass out?"

"Fuck you think she did? Yeah, she threw my ass out. Why the fuck did you have to go to her? I told you I would handle everything when I was ready to."

"And when was that going to be, huh? When the baby was born? His first birthday? Oh, wait, maybe when he graduates high school, he'll be eighteen and no longer your responsibility!"

"C'mon with that shit, T. You makin' my fuckin' dick go soft with all that crazy talk. Ain't no need for that when you pregnant."

"Oh, please! Don't act like you give a fuck about me and this baby now after you fired me! That's why I went to your house and told your wife about us! You told me she was the reason why you had to let me go. To my surprise, she had no fuckin' clue about me or our baby! What happened to you telling her? All that shit was a lie! All you do is lie, Cap!"

I sighed while tightening my fists. "You're right, I lied. I shouldn't have done that to you, okay? I just need some time to figure out all this shit."

"What is there to figure out? I'm having your baby, Cap!"

"And she's my wife, Tia!"

"She's always been your wife, Cap. She's been your wife since long before I fuckin' met you, but that ain't stop you from puttin' your dick inside me, right?"

I clenched my jaws. "Look, dead all that shit. You stepped outta line with what you did today, Tia. I tell you like I tell anybody else; I don't give a fuck what I'm out here doin'. My kids and my wife are off fuckin' limits."

She huffed while pointing to her stomach. "And what about this kid, huh?"

"My son will be well taken care of."

"Yeah, while he lives here with me, his daddy lives up in the house on the hill with his queen and little princesses. I don't even have a job to provide for him! You took that from me!"

"You don't have to work, Tia. Taking care of my son right now means taking care of you because you're carrying him. You're carrying my baby boy," I said, reaching out for her stomach.

She pressed her lips together, and I could tell she'd loosened up her tense body a bit because I felt the baby kick. "He knows who his daddy is," she told me.

I licked my lips and brushed my hand against her cheek. "And what about you? Do you know who Daddy is?"

Tia looked up into the puppy dog stare I gave her and practically melted in my hands like putty. She smiled when I pulled her lips onto mine to seal the deal.

"I'm going out of town for the weekend on business, but I'm gon' deposit some money into your account tonight, okay? Don't worry, Daddy's got both of you," I promised her.

As soon as I turned to leave, my phone vibrated in my pocket. I quickly pulled it out, hoping not to see Hermès' name across the screen. My breathing relaxed as soon as I saw it was my client, Rio.

"This is Julius Capone," I answered.

"Yo, Cap. I got your retainer fee plus a lil somethin' extra for good measure. Where you at? Let's link up before I head down to the club."

I smiled at the sound of new money coming my way. "I'm headed out of town for the weekend, but you can drop it off at my house. I'll text you the address, and you can just leave it there for me."

"This ain't no lemonade stand money, Cap. This big bread. You sure you want me to leave that shit on your doorstep?"

"I live in a gated community, trust me. I'll give the gatekeeper your name so you can drive in, then ring the doorbell and drop it off. We good?" I asked before ending the call.

"Yeah, we good. Just send me your address and shit, and I'll get it taken care of."

"Coming your way," I said and ended the call.

## CHAPTER 4

# The Unexpected Guest

**Hermès**

My husband was gone. My girls were upstairs asleep. Where was I? Sitting in the dark, letting the light from the electric fireplace illuminate the living room. I had an overfilled glass of merlot glued to my hands and mascara stains down my cheeks as I stared at my favorite picture of Cap and me on our wedding day six years prior.

He hadn't had the decency to tell me he was sorry for being the cause of my pain. I was mad at myself for even thinking that much of him. He didn't seem to know anything when it came to who he wanted or how he felt about the mess he'd made. Cap had never been a man who couldn't make a decision. He was a boss and at one time, I was his one and only lady. I never minded sharing the spotlight with our daughters, but I would be damned if I shared it with another woman and her bastard. The truth was, I didn't know how to live in a world that didn't involve being Julius Capone's wife, but somehow, I was going to have to get back to how I used to be before I ever met him, independent as fuck.

The doorbell chimed throughout the house's lower half, and my body jolted forward. Drops of wine jumped out of my glass and onto the dark wood-stained floor.

"Shit," I mumbled.

I looked at my phone to check the time. It was ten-forty-two p.m. My heart quickened as my feet slowly dragged over to the door.

"Who is it?"

"Rio."

"Who?"

"Nario. I'm one of Cap's clients."

"Cap isn't here," I said through the door.

"I just need to drop off his bread, that's it," he replied.

"Can you come back some other time?"

"It's just money. I ain't on no bullshit. You can even call him if you want. How you think I got in the gate?"

I gently rested my hand against the door while the other gripped the doorknob. "Give me a minute."

I quickly deactivated the security alarm and cracked the door to see him wearing a black V-neck t-shirt that showed a sneak peek of the tattoo etched into his collarbone and two gold chains around his neck. I noticed he was holding a manila envelope that had been folded in half.

"Why you lookin' like that? Do I scare you that much?" he asked me, referring to the scowl on my face.

"No, it's just...how'd you know where we live?"

"Cap told me to drop the money off tonight and gave me the address. I ain't know he ain't tell you I was comin'."

"That ain't the only thing he don't tell me," I muttered without realizing the words were fleeing past my lips. "I'm sorry..."

"Nah, you good."

"You said you had some money for my husband?"

"Yeah, tell 'em it's all right here," he said, extending the envelope to me.

I nodded and then gave him another once-over. This time, looking at him more carefully. He looked like a mixture between a boss and a bad boy, from the dark waves flooding his head down to the sparkling chains around his neck. Whoever he was, he was the perfect storm; nice to look at from a distance, but dangerous as hell if he got too close.

I reached out to take the envelope and let my fingertips gently brush over the top of his hand. My instincts quickly made me draw my arm back. "I'm sorry...again."

"Stop apologizing," he told me with a serious look on his face.

"I didn't mean to interrupt your meeting with my husband...I just —I'm s—yeah."

"You don't have to explain shit to me..."

"Hermès."

The corners of his lips upturned. "Hermès, like the God of wealth and luck."

I wanted to smile back at him, but the dried tear streaks on my cheeks made it harder to make facial expressions of happiness or joy, even laughter.

"Yeah..."

"Well, like I said, you don't have to explain shit to me, Hermès."

The way my name fell off his tongue made me clench the doorknob tighter. His beard looked soft to the touch, but I kept my hands to myself.

"I know this is going to sound weird and probably even inappropriate, but would you like to come in?"

His eyebrows lifted toward his forehead as he licked his lips. "You sure that's a good idea?"

"You were the one who said you weren't on no bullshit, right?" I said, throwing his words back at him.

He cracked a slight smile that almost blinded me. I quickly took my eyes down to the floor.

"You don't strike me as the lonely housewife type."

I shrugged. "I didn't strike myself as a lot of things before today."

Instead of responding, he turned away and pulled out his keys. I watched him walk toward his running engine and get inside the car. I couldn't tell what kind of car it was, but the way the engine purred, I could tell it was luxury. My heart tinged. Two men had rejected me in one day, and I wasn't even trying to sleep with him. Just before I closed the door and sulked back over to my pit in the middle of the couch, I heard the engine shut off and the doors lock. My head swung back up to see him walking back in my direction with something in his hand.

He stepped back onto the front porch and flashed a bottle of Hennessy at me. "If I'm comin' in, I'm drinkin'," he told me.

And then it happened. Laughter. Not gut-wrenching, knee-slapping laughter. Just laughter after I thought I'd never smile through the pain again.

"Okay then."

I closed the door behind him, and he followed me back into the dark living room. I turned on the lights beside the couch, and he sat in the chair across from me.

"So, what's your story?" I asked, picking up where I'd left off with my glass of wine.

"What do you mean?" he asked, sipping his Hennessy straight from the bottle.

"I can get you a glass."

He nodded. "Thank you."

I hopped up and walked into the kitchen. I stood on the tips of my toes and reached for a glass out of the cabinet. For a second, I questioned myself. *What the hell am I doing?* I thought. There could never be a valid reason for the wife of a criminal defense attorney to be kickin' it with his client. Holding the glass in my hand, I returned to the living room.

"What were you sayin'?" he asked me.

"I asked you what your story was. You know, like, what did you do to land yourself in my husband's company?"

He threw the liquor in his glass back with one toss as if it was as tasteless as water. "Someone I may have been seen with on occasion got caught up and opened his mouth to say some shit he shouldn't have. Cops showed up at my crib with a search warrant. They thought they were gon' find shit, and all they found was my gun."

"Was it registered?"

"Yeah, to somebody. The serial number was altered."

I nodded. "I'm sorry, I didn't mean to be so much into your business."

"I'm a black man in a white man's America. It don't matter if it was registered to me or not. In their eyes, I'm just another monkey they gettin' off the street to put in a cage."

"How much time are you looking at for something like that?"

"Since this ain't my first time in court, Cap said I'm lookin' at anywhere from a nine to ten-year bid and hefty ass fine."

"Jesus! I can't even imagine."

"I caught a case, and now I have a lawyer. I'm good. I've never been afraid of goin' to jail."

"I just can't imagine being away from my girls that long. Don't you feel a way about having to leave the people you love?"

"People like who?"

"I mean, where's your girl or wife?"

"Ain't nobody to leave behind. I'm single, and I ain't got no kids, at least none that I know about."

I scoffed. "I find that hard to believe."

"Which part?"

"I don't know...you just seem slick...like a player. It's like you tell me what you think I wanna hear, but not the truth."

He smirked. "So, you want me to be single, huh?"

I looked him up and down and then took a sip from my glass before softly chuckling. "Real funny."

Rio clutched his chest as if he felt some type of way. "Damn. You ain't never heard the saying don't judge a book by its cover?"

"Yeah, I have."

Rio leaned in towards me. "Then stop judging me until you get to know me," he whispered.

His voice made my spine shiver.

"I'm just saying, it seems like nowadays all men do is cheat."

"There you go again. That's not true, Hermès."

"So, you're telling me you've never cheated?" I quizzed.

"Nah, I'm not saying that. But just because I fucked up in the past doesn't make me a worthless ass nigga."

I shrugged and shifted in my seat.

"I guess."

"So, you're perfect?"

"I didn't say that."

He looked over at me. "It's my turn now, right?"

"Yeah, I guess so." I shrugged.

"So, what you doing sitting here with a big ass ring sitting on the table instead of wrapped around your finger?" he asked.

"Wow, that's mighty personal for a stranger to ask, don't you think?"

"Hey, I have an inquiring mind just like you."

I sighed as I leaned forward to pour myself a fresh glass and set the bottle beside my three-point-five-carat halo-cut diamond wedding ring.

"Damn, is it that bad?" he asked, pointing at my ring with just his eyes.

"If you didn't notice, I wasn't in the best mood earlier today," I replied.

"I think everybody noticed that."

"Now I'm stuck going back and forth in my head over this shit. Do I stay or do I go?"

Before he had a chance to respond, I cut him off. "I feel like such a crazy person for even talking to you about this. You're the last person I should be seeking advice from, but on the other hand, you're the only other adult here, and this sure as hell beats talking to myself."

Silence hung between us as he stared at me with such intensity behind his eyes. I felt almost paralyzed under his gaze. I didn't want to move a muscle until he spoke.

"I don't think you're crazy, Hermès. I think you're human."

I exhaled loudly in relief. "I feel like an alien who has landed on another planet watching this bad, bootleg, alternative version of my life. As real as I know it is, it all feels like one big, bad fuckin' dream."

Every time I spoke, the room went silent as if I was only speaking to hear myself talk. Talking to Rio began to feel like I was talking to a handsome brick wall.

"Can you please say something? If I'm the only one talking, this isn't much of a two-way conversation."

"What do you want?"

"Excuse me?"

"You heard me. What do you want?"

I shook my head, unable to remember the last time someone had asked me what it was that I wanted. "I don't know—of course, I want my children to be safe and live happy lives. I—"

"Not for your children, Hermès. For you."

I shrugged at a loss. "I think that answer is too complicated for words."

"Then make it simple."

Silence hung between us for a few seconds before I parted my lips to speak. "Love. Real, true love."

"That's all?"

"Isn't that enough? Cap never learned to love me, at least not how I loved him."

"You gon' give him another chance?"

I looked at the stranger in my living room with tears rimming my lower lash line, ready to fall at any given second. I swiped at them while looking away. "Another chance to do what? Break my heart again? You think this is the first time I've heard whispers of him cheating? It's not. But no one was ever brave enough to step to me, let alone come straight to my doorstep. I'd be a fool if I ignored it this time. I've drawn many lines over a million times, and they never seem to make a difference. I already know the possibility of me ever loving again is slim to none, but I don't want my daughters growing up without their father around."

"You don't have to stay with the nigga for him to be around his kids. If he's a real man, he'll take care of his responsibilities whether he under the same roof as them or not."

"You said you don't have kids, right?"

"Nah, no kids."

"So, you wouldn't understand."

"I don't have to be a father to know what it feels like to grow up in a house without one," he cut back. "there's a difference between a nigga who wanna be a father and one who don't, that's all I'm sayin'."

I swallowed the growing lump in my throat and decided to change the subject. "What time is it?"

We both glanced down at my phone simultaneously, and I tapped the screen to illuminate it with the time. "Wow, I didn't realize it was so late. It's almost midnight."

"You about to call it a night?" he asked.

"Yeah, you?"

"No, the night is just getting started for me. I own a nightclub downtown."

"A nightclub? What's the name of it?"

"The Underground."

"Wow...that must be stressful."

He shrugged. "Sometimes, but I don't stress easily."

"Well, that makes one of us," I said, laughing at my weakness.

"I should let you get to the rest of your busy night."

Rio stood to his feet and watched me stand to mine before walking toward the front door. "Thanks for the drink."

"Thanks for the talk. You're a good listener."

"I try to live by the notion that we got two ears and only one mouth for a reason."

I shot him a surprised glance and then nodded. "Wise notion."

"Goodnight, Hermès."

"Goodnight."

I closed the door behind him and leaned my back against it. My head was swimming, and I didn't know if it was the wine getting to me or him. The more he talked, the more I became fascinated with the mystery behind his eyes. I knew there was more than he was letting on with his pending court date, but I didn't want to press him. I had no intentions of making a new friend, but Rio had quickly become the forbidden fruit my lips desired to taste. *Eat your heart out, Eve,* I thought to myself.

### Nario 'Rio' Sullivan

I backed out of the long driveway and headed downtown. It was the first time the sky had been dark enough to see the stars above me. I'd spent all thirty-four years of my life living under the bright lights and the hustle and bustle of Philly and never once saw a star. My eyes strayed away from the road ahead and down to my vibrating phone.

"Hello?"

"Yo, Rio. Where the fuck you at, nigga?" my boy Vez asked me.

"I'm on my way to the club now. I had to handle somethin' that took me a little out the way, but I'm comin'."

"Good, because we need to talk..."

I nodded, knowing what he was referring to without him having to complete his sentence. "We'll do that when I get there," I assured him.

I hung up the phone, thinking Hermès was wrong. Running a club wasn't the stressful part; it was everything else around it that caught my head in a whirlwind. Not only was I dealing with a court case that could land my ass in prison for up to a decade, but I was also dealing with an anaconda in my own garden. Being unexpectedly pulled into some bullshit made me realize I should've been lookin' closer to home when I was thinkin' about mothafuckas who wanted to see me fall.

The first thing I did when the cops burst through my door was vow that I was going to silence whoever set me up permanently. The second thing I did was hire a lawyer. I'd been watching Cap's moves in the news about how he was able to get a lot of niggas time reduced or their entire case dropped. His services came with a hefty price tag that I didn't mind as long as I got off. I had no idea a man with that much weight in the justice system would be a sucker, but then again, I didn't judge niggas. I just knew what box to put him in. Any man who cheated knowing he had a woman who looked as good as Hermès did was a straight clown in my eyes.

I'd only been around her for a little over an hour, but her presence was refreshing. She wasn't one of those pathetic ass, no self-worth havin' bitches that flocked to niggas with a lil change in their pockets. She was just a good girl stuck with a clown-ass nigga. Unfortunately for her, I was worse than him. I had no intention of saving her from him or herself. As I pulled up to my reserved spot in front of the club, I placed my thoughts and opinions about her to the back of my head and headed inside.

The familiar scent of sweat and Hennessy wafted past my nose as I walked through the sea of people trying to smoke, drink, and dance their problems away. My eyes caught Vez staring at me from a few feet away, and I already knew what was up. He and I made millions off the corner together and graduated from nobodies in the game to the niggas runnin' it. An attack on me meant an attack on him, and neither of us was ready to give up the lives we never thought we'd have.

He dapped me up and pulled me into him. "It's about time you got here."

I brushed him off. "Let's go to the back."

I slid the key to my office out of my pocket and unlocked the door. As soon as Vez closed the door behind him, he spoke up. "I know who snitched."

"Say his name then."

"That nigga Carlo. I did some diggin' and heard he got picked up by the feds a couple of weeks before them niggas kicked in your door and shit."

"That was around the same time that nigga called talkin' 'bout he was goin' out of town to bury his cousin."

Vez huffed. "Exactly. I say we handle his rat ass tonight. The nigga can't testify if he ain't breathin'."

"As much as I wanna see that nigga's brains splattered all over his dash, we gotta put that shit on ice for now."

"What?" Vez asked, scrunching up his forehead.

"You heard me. I'm going to look more suspect if the nigga turn up missing. Let's just let that nigga Cap do his thing."

"That's that new lawyer nigga you workin' with? You sure you can trust 'em?"

"He's being paid a lot of money to be trustworthy. Besides, he has as much to lose in this as I do, so I'm sure he'll be more inclined to work his magic."

Vez nodded. "Bet."

"Once he puts them boys back to sleep for me, we can talk about handlin' Carlo. It's a shame these bitch ass niggas gotta learn the hard way."

"Niggas see a lil green and get too excited."

"And then what comes after the excitement? Fuck ups. The number one shit you don't say when you get caught hittin' a lick is my mothafuckin name."

"That bitch ass nigga is a pig with no badge," Vez mumbled.

"You just make sure none of my niggas make a move until after this shit is done, all right? When the time comes, I'm gonna cut that nigga's tongue out for disrespectin' me."

I hated how it seemed like the bigger I got, the more niggas couldn't wait for the bus to come so they could throw me under it. I only trusted the niggas who ate at the table with me, but Carlo was more than my nigga. He was my cousin. As much as that shit broke my heart, I knew he was going to have to be dealt with as if he was a stranger off the corner.

## CHAPTER 5

# Hit 'em Up Style

**Hermès**

I woke up the following day with my body starfished across the couch. It was the best sleep I'd gotten in the past few days. I supposed I had the half-finished bottle of wine on the coffee table to thank for that. My ears perked up when I heard the girls descending the stairs at full force.

"Mommy, mommy," Symphony squealed in her light, airy voice.

"Good morning, baby," I said while stretching my limbs. "Are you two ready for some breakfast?"

I fluffed out the couch pillows that were indented from me, laying on them, then quickly swiped up the bottle of wine and two glasses. Holding Rio's glass in my hand made me smile a little. For a second, I thought that his visit may have been a dream. I would've never invited a strange man into my home had it not been for the liquid courage I'd been sipping on before he rang my doorbell.

As soon as I put the dishes in the sink, I heard Melody's voice behind me.

"Mama, what's this?"

I turned to see her holding the large envelope filled with money in her tiny hands. My eyes widened before I walked over to take it from her. "Thank you. I'll take it."

"What is it?"

"It's...money."

"Whose money?" Symphony quizzed.

I sighed. She was so curious at her age. "It's our money," I said, opening the envelope and fingering through the oversized stack of one-hundred-dollar bills.

"Damn," I mumbled. I could practically smell the fresh blue-faced bills through the envelope.

"Ooooh, Mommy! You said a bad word! You can't say a bad word!" Symphony reprimanded me.

"I'm sorry, princess. Mommy will put money in the swear jar."

I handed her a brown-spotted banana to peel while I cut up apple slices for her sister. Once that was done, I poured cereal into their bowls and waited for my piece of toast to pop up from the toaster. Warm water and iridescent soap flowed over my hands as I washed the few dishes in the sink. Once the girls were fed, I swiped the crumbs from the toaster into the sink and scrubbed the stovetop with a worn dish sponge. I tossed it alongside the empty wine bottle into the trashcan.

* * *

Two hours later, the house smelled like fresh laundry and baked cookies. The girls were dressed and playing with their doll babies in the middle of the living room floor. I swiped my purse off the table and kissed the tops of their heads.

"Let's go."

"Where are we going, Mommy?" Symphony asked.

"Shopping."

I took one last look at the pictures of my happily ever after sprawled all over the walls before closing the door. I'd dedicated my life to my family, doing whatever I felt was needed to be done for everyone to be happy. Someone had rewritten my story without my permission, and it was time I did something for myself. I shoved the envelope into my purse and took it as compensation for my hurt feelings.

Later that day, I'd spent half the envelope on clothes and toys for the girls and new jewelry and bags for myself.

"I don't know about you, but Mommy is hungry. What do you say, girls? Let's go get dinner," I said as I slammed down the trunk lid filled with dozens of designer shopping bags.

By the time we got home, Cap's car was pulled up in the driveway. I quickly looked in my rearview mirror at the girls. They were knocked out. As long as I could get them in the house and keep them asleep, they wouldn't slip up and tell their father about our little girl's day out, and I could keep the bags in the trunk overnight.

I walked through the door with both girls in my arms and saw a bouquet of long-stemmed red roses in a vase in the foyer. Instead of stopping, I put the girls in their beds upstairs. I slid my heels off my feet before prancing back downstairs, only to see Cap standing at the bottom with his arms folded across his chest.

"Did you see the flowers I got you?"

"Didn't know they were for me."

His forehead creased. "Of course, they were for you. Who else would they be for?"

I rolled my eyes. "I saw them, Cap."

"You like them?"

"They nice," I said, smacking my lips together.

He inched forward to me, and I backed away as if he were a stranger. His posture stiffened, freezing his barrel-chested frame in place. Instead of saying anything else, he brushed past me and walked upstairs. I didn't care if I'd hurt his feelings. If he thought a bouquet of roses was a sufficient enough apology for a side bitch and a kid, he was sadly mistaken. I just wasn't in the mood to cry over him anymore. He didn't deserve my tears.

## Nario 'Rio' Sullivan

. . .

It'd been a week, and I hadn't gotten an update on my case from Cap, so I told him to meet me at Lucky's Pool Hall and Pub downtown. I tossed the last bit of the Henny in my glass down my throat as I eyed him, walking between the rows of occupied pool tables. He stepped over and dapped me up before leaning against the wall next to the rack. His body language told me his ass was too comfortable around me, and I was gon' have to check that.

"What up?" he asked.

"Shit. You good?"

"I'm all right. Why'd you want me to meet you here instead of my office?"

"Are you uncomfortable?"

"Never that."

"Good. You play pool?" I asked.

"Sure. Rack 'em."

"You wanna play a nine, ten, or fifteen ball game?"

"Fifteen is cool."

"Get comfortable, nigga. Next drink on me. What you drinkin'?"

"Henny is cool," he said, hanging his suit jacket on the wall rack.

I waved the waitress down and watched as he loosened his tie. "Oh, I see you already got your game face on, nigga."

"I never take it off," he told me.

I scraped the blue chalk cube on the tip of my pool stick before smacking the balls across the table, sending three of them into different pockets. "That's funny because neither do I."

"Nice shot," he said, sipping his drink.

The TV blared in the background against the repetitive crack of the shiny balls knocking into each other on the table. Cap hit the eleven ball with a satisfying smack and looked up at me.

"Why'd you call me here, Rio? Don't bullshit me."

I sat on the table's edge with my stick in one hand and my drink in the other. "You know, I was raised to never trust a nigga."

"That's funny because so was I," he replied.

"Why haven't I heard from you about my case then, nigga?"

"You know I speak money first before anything. Where is mine?"

"Fuck you talkin' about? I gave it to your bitch at your crib like you told me to, so don't talk to me. Talk to her. I held up my end of this shit, now it's your turn."

"When the fuck did you see my wife?"

I chuckled. "Shit, me and Hermès go way back."

He stepped closer to me. "Never let me hear my wife's name fall off your tongue again. She ain't got shit to do with none of this."

"She does if she got my fuckin' money."

"I'll check with her about it, aight?"

"You do that. My money has already changed hands once, so if you can't handle it, let me know now so I can cut all ties. You know how I do that, right?"

"No need for threats, nigga."

I leaned into him. "Let me let you in on something I'm not sure you know. I was born with a talent for violence and terror. I run Philly from the south to uptown. I don't give a fuck who you are. You don't run me. I speak about who I want when the fuck I want."

Cap set his lips in a hard line before nodding. "I told you I'd ask about it. I'll get back to you."

"And when you do, make sure you got an update on my case, nigga."

"I will," he assured me.

"In case you forgot, it was your drug connect that started all this shit, so if I go down, who the fuck else you think is goin' down?"

"Aight, I told you I fuckin' got it. Chill the fuck out," he said as he popped a piece of gum in his mouth, trying to mask the smell of cognac on his breath.

I was raised never to trust another nigga, especially one who worked on the opposite side of the law. If he couldn't keep his home life together, I didn't know how he planned to handle my situation, but every time he came to me empty-handed, I was gon' remind his ass he had a lot more to lose than just his wife.

## CHAPTER 6

# *The XXX Factor*

### Hermès

I'd successfully gotten all the new merchandise I bought into the house, put it away, and tossed the shopping bags in the recycling bin and out on the curb without hearing a peep from Cap about the money. He came storming through the door smelling like Black and Mild's and cheap liquor.

"Hermès! Hermès!" he yelled throughout the lower half of the house.

"Kitchen," I yelled back. "Stop yelling before you wake the girls up!"

Cap darted into the kitchen so fast that he almost hit his head on the hanging rack with pots and pans dangling. "Where's the money, Hermès?"

I frowned. "What money?"

"You know exactly what money I'm talking about. I already know what the fuck is going on, so you might as well come clean! Rio told me he dropped off a lump sum to you when I was out of town."

I rolled my eyes and sighed. "I may have taken some and invested it."

His forehead creased. "Invested it? In what?"

"A new wardrobe for me and the girls."

His eyes widened with fury. "Are you fuckin' kidding me? Take all that shit back and get me my money!"

"I can't."

"What do you mean you can't? You can and you will! First thing in the morning!"

"I tossed all the bags, receipts, and tags," I admitted.

Cap slammed his fists down on the granite countertop, and I jumped. "Fuck!" he roared.

"It's just money, Cap. Look around you. We have plenty."

"You don't know what the fuck you just did," he snarled.

"Then tell me. Maybe I can help."

"You mothafuckin right you'll help," he said, yanking me by my arm.

Cap pulled me upstairs into our oversized bedroom closet. He didn't let go until he got to the safe, put in the code, and opened the fire-proof door. Inside were stacks on stacks of money piled neatly on top of each other.

My eyes widened. "Cap, what the fuck is all of this? Where did all of this money come from?"

"I don't keep all our money in the bank."

"Why not?"

"Insurance policy," he told me. "Did you spend it all?"

"No. There's some left."

"How fuckin' much?"

I shrugged nervously. "I don't know—maybe a couple thousand."

"Go get it!"

I darted out of the closet and went to pull the envelope out from underneath a picture keepsake box underneath the bed. I spread all the money out on the bed and counted it.

Cap walked out and tossed ten stacks on the bed. "How much is left?"

"A little over two thousand."

"This should cover it."

"What the fuck is going on, Cap? What the fuck are you into with him? And what does any of this have to do with me?"

"You're gon' take your ass down to his club and give it to him. You tell him you're sorry for what you did and that you put a little extra inside to settle anything you may have started between me and him."

"Wait a minute, did he threaten you, Cap? Why don't you drop him as a client if he threatened you?"

"He ain't threaten me, all right? This is just how we do business. Now, pick out somethin' sexy and put it on. You're takin' your ass down there tonight!"

"Why can't you call and tell him you have his money? Why do I have to go?"

"You did this! You put this family in danger, Hermès! Not me! You are gonna be the one to fix this shit. Now put this shit in your purse and go get dressed, I'll text you the address."

* * *

An hour and a half later, I was dripping in designer from head to toe with over ten thousand dollars in cash stuffed inside my purse. My hands shook as I drove past the club entrance to check it out. There was a line of people waiting outside to be let in. Girls in their short dresses and men standing under clouds of cigarette and weed smoke, trying to get their buzz before walking inside. I circled the block three times before finding a vacant parking spot that didn't require me to walk three miles in five-inch stiletto heels.

When I stepped inside, my nostrils detected a whiff of weed smoke beneath the smell of a good time. After hitting the bar, I sat at a small round table with a shot glass and a lime wedge on the edge. I needed all the liquid courage I could get to go through with what Cap asked me to do. There were bottles of liquor lining the mirrored wall behind the bar, so if the tequila in my glass didn't work, I had plenty of other options. I screwed up my face at the bold taste of tequila flowing down my throat and swiped my hair behind my ear. It had been so long since I'd been out in Philly's night scene. The bass from the speakers vibrated the chair underneath me.

As I looked around, I fanned my hand past my dewy forehead, trying to cool myself down from the hot, stuffy air. Clusters of people hung out together and danced in their social circles. Girls stood on the outskirts of the dance floor taking selfies, and men checked them out from afar like wolves, waiting for the perfect chance to attack their prey. My eyes caught Rio standing amongst the sea of people, and my heart rate sped up. Although surrounded, he stood out like the beautiful sore thumb he was. No one around him even came close to being able to take my attention away even for a second. I stared at him until he locked eyes with me. I cowardly looked away. A few seconds passed before I drew enough courage to look back, and he was gone. My eyes fell back toward the dance floor until I felt a tap on my shoulder.

"You drink hard liquor?"

I shrugged. "I needed something stronger than wine to do what I'm about to do."

"You got somethin' for me?"

I nodded. "I do."

"That nigga sent you?"

I lowered my eyes. "It seems I owe you an apology."

"You mothafuckin right you do."

"I'm sorry for getting in between whatever business you have with my husband. I never should've taken my issues with him out on you— or your money."

"How much did you spend?"

"Over half of it, but I've got it all back for you. It's here in my purse," I said, pulling my bag off my shoulder.

Rio placed his hand on top of mine to stop me. "Not here."

I nodded. "Okay..."

"Follow me to the back."

* * *

## Rio

I stayed two paces ahead of her to watch her walk to me while I stood at my office door. She began to walk toward me, and time stood still. I licked my lips as she swiped her long, flowing hair behind her ear. She looked up at me, and her eyes twinkled underneath the flashing club lights. When she stepped up to me, I turned to unlock the door, and she followed me inside.

"Now, you were saying?" I asked, leaning against my desk.

Her shoulders sagged. "I'm sorry, Rio. That isn't who I am. It had everything to do with him and nothing to do with you, and I apologize."

"What all did Cap tell you to get you to come here?"

She shook her head. "Nothing."

"I thought we were friends. You don't lie to friends, Hermès."

"Look, I don't want to get in between whatever you have going on with my husband. I don't know anything, okay? Can you please just take the money back so I can leave? I want to get home to my kids."

I surveyed her demeanor closely. "Tell me the truth about this next question, and you can go."

"Okay, what is it?"

"Why'd you take my money?"

She sighed. "I wanted to get back at him for doin' me so dirty, you know? I don't know. There's still a part of me that keeps wishing that tomorrow will be the day I wake up, and my family is put back together. I keep not wanting this to be real."

Her honesty made me stand straight up. It was raw, pure. I knew no woman as beautiful and as good as her had any business being with a nigga like Cap. She deserved a nigga who would treat her and her body right. I could most definitely do the second.

"You remember when I told you I owned this club?" I asked.

She nodded. "Yeah. What about it?"

"There's another section here. A private one."

"Private?"

"It's invite only. I call it *The Vault*. Only the heavy hitters in the city and from all over can afford to enter."

"What happens in there?" she asked.

"Anything they want to. As long as their money is green, the possibilities are endless."

"So, you basically allow women to prostitute in there instead of on the streets?" she asked, turning up her nose at me.

I shook my head. "Nah. It's nothin' like that. It's where I met your husband, in fact."

She turned her brows down at me. "What was he doing here?"

"What do you think?"

"So, you knew he was cheating on me the moment you met me?"

I nodded. "I did."

She rolled her eyes while folding her arms across her chest. "Wow..."

"Have you seen him do anything with other women?"

"I can't tell you that, and even if I could, I wouldn't. Your heart can't take that shit."

"You said it's private, right? Like, members only?"

"Yeah."

"How long has Cap been a member?"

"Almost a year now."

"How do you become a member?"

"You pay the fee."

"How much is it?"

"Twenty bands a year."

Her lips parted in surprise. "What if I want to try it out before becoming a member?"

"Entrance fee is a thousand dollars."

"Sign me up then. I want to see what it's about."

"If this has anything to do with why my marriage fell apart, I think I have a right to see what the hype is about!"

"I can tell you're not open-minded enough to find out."

"Yes, I am."

"Nah, sweetheart. You not."

"What makes you say that? If I'm tellin' you I wanna see it, then I wanna see it, Rio."

I looked her up and down. "If you ready, come back tomorrow at midnight, and I'll pay your entrance fee."

"Midnight? Why so late?"

"You ever heard the sayin' freaks come out at night? Well, I'm as freaky as they fuckin' come. I don't know if you're ready for all *The Vault* has to offer you, both mentally and physically."

"I'll be here...tomorrow at midnight," she said as she smoothed her hands down the front of her skintight black dress.

A smile tugged at my lips. "You just make sure you keep that same energy when you step inside tomorrow."

She nodded, emptied her purse on my desk, and turned to leave. I ran my hands down my jaw as I watched her until the door separated her presence from mine. When I met her, something told me to run fast and far in the opposite direction, but instead, I'd run smack into her. Lettin' pussy come between the business arrangement Cap, and I had was dangerous as fuck for me, but there was no way I could stay away.

## CHAPTER 7

# *The Vault*

**Hermès**

I smoothed the palms of my hands down the front of my bodycon cherry red dress as I walked into Rio's club entrance. As soon as the bartender handed me my drink, Rio appeared.

"You showed," he said.

"I told you I would."

"Are you ready?"

I nodded before taking a sip of my drink. "Yeah."

"C'mon then, let's go."

Rio held his hand out to me, and I followed him down the hallway and into an elevator.

"Why *The Vault* for a name?" I asked.

"The lower half of this building used to be a bank. Plus, everybody alive got a vault. It's where we keep all our fantasies, kinks and shit. *The Vault* is where people get to live an uninhibited lifestyle. Life stops when you step inside. There are no responsibilities. The only thing on everyone's mind is pleasure."

"No offense, but I thought you were just some sort of drug dealer. I had no idea any of this even existed."

"I'm a freak, Hermès. I love to fuck. Why not open up somethin' I love and get paid for it?"

"How do people even find something like this? As soon as I got home last night, I Googled it. There's no online presence about anything related to *The Vault*."

"Private is private to anyone that wasn't meant to know. People can explore their fantasies in peace. It's upscale, safe and secure. I tune mothafuckas into what turns them on. Anything from Minor kink to extreme BDSM."

"Wow..."

"When we're good, we're good, but when mothafuckas allow themselves to be bad, we're so much better."

"What about those with wives?"

"I told you it's a private community. Anything goes. As long as the money stays green, I don't judge."

"So, anyone can just do anything they want?"

"Just about, but every party has rules that can't be broken," he told me.

My heart rate sped up every time his eyes locked with mine. My eyes couldn't wait to see what was behind the elevator doors. The second the box dinged, the doors opened, and my brain instantly started recording everything my eyes drew in. The cold concrete walls were dark and inviting. There were two levels, the top being all private rooms while the bottom had a dance club atmosphere. As we descended the stairs, I saw a more open layout where people were chatting with glasses of champagne in their hands while wearing black lingerie and leather masks. It was all free, yet one big secret to the outside world.

"C'mon, I wanna show you something," Rio said, grabbing my hand and leading me toward the left side of the room.

We stopped in front of a large observation window and watched a white couple in the middle of a scene. The walls were padded in tufted red leather. She wore black fishnet stockings, a lace mask, and black tassels on her nipples. She was being restrained on a chair with her ass in the air. The man wore a black leather gas mask with a whip in his hand.

"Slap me harder!" she yelled.

"I want you to beg for it with my dick in your mouth."

"Slap me! Please, Daddy!" she said before he stuffed her open mouth.

"Mmm, I can already tell you're going to know my whip very well," he told her.

I watched him untie her from the chair and sit down himself while bending her over his knee and spanking her some more. "Tell Daddy how happy I make you."

"He's teaching her obedience," Rio told me without taking his eyes off them.

"By smacking her?"

"All play is consensual, and if things get out of hand or uncomfortable, they have a safe word."

"Do you have a safe word?"

"Yeah."

"What is it?"

"If I tell you that, I gotta show you how to use it..."

I swallowed hard while clenching my thighs together. "Oh..."

"It's ecstasy," he whispered in my ear.

We walked down further and saw porn playing on a projector while a middle-aged white man sat naked with his legs spread wide and dick standing at attention as he watched his wife have the time of her life while riding the dick of a younger black man.

"Mmm, shit. His dick feels so good, Winston."

"Tell your bitch how good she looks," the black man said while smacking the woman's ass.

"You're so beautiful, baby," Winston told her.

"Grab my hair and fuck me like a dog!" she screamed.

Rio smiled. "I like to call that reparations."

Winston continued to sit there watching while his wife got pleasured while never touching either of them. It was almost as if they weren't even married. Rio and I watched as they switched positions, and she started riding him in the reverse cowgirl position while placing her foot on her husband's head.

"Don't move, Winston," she commanded.

Rio leaned in and whispered in my ear. "Believe it or not, there are lots of couples who join together."

"And have sex with other people?"

"Sometimes, or just even with each other."

We continued to walk until stopping to watch a younger couple lying next to each other on a red velvet couch. She rubbed her nipples as she got turned out by a female while some other girl rode her husband's dick.

"Is this turning you on?" Rio asked, eyeing me closely.

"I don't know what it's doing, honestly."

"What turns you on, Hermès?"

"I—I don't know," I answered, shying away from his question.

He smiled. "Walk around and get comfortable. When you find out, you come find me."

He was right. His freak level was unmatched. I kept walking and saw a woman sucking dick through a glory hole in a room decorated with mirrors everywhere. The more I walked, the more unspeakable acts I saw. There were women locked in cages wearing black lace blindfolds with thin leather whips clenched between their teeth as they swayed their hips from side to side.

I half expected all the members to be naked, but most kept it classy with lingerie made from the finest silks or business attire.

* * *

By the next hour, I'd seen threesomes and foursomes of people in rooms decorated like the perfect vacation to the tropics, a night in Paris, Arabia, and Brazil. They were a train of bodies licking and sticking for pleasure. I'd seen partners tag each other in and out of group sex play, men giving men blowjobs, and women giving men blowjobs all in the same room. Being a peeping Tom made me feel awkward. Casually walking through a sea of sex was ultimately out of my element. I stood frozen in front of two of the most beautiful women I'd ever seen while going to the bar. They looked like supermodels with eyes all on them as if they were the center of attention.

One slid the strap on after sucking the tip. She made the other suck on it before bending her over. She rubbed the dick up and down her pussy, getting it nice and wet, and then slid it in.

"Mmm, shit," she moaned.

The one being penetrated was lying on her back with her right leg in the air while the other lay beside her. I watched them kiss as she thrust into her. It was so soft and sensual that I could feel the passion between them with every moan.

"Would you like to join us?" one asked me.

"We'll make you cum better than a dick ever could," the other added.

"No thank you…"

"No pressure. The offer will always be on the table…"

I scurried out of their view, made my way over to the bar, and sat down.

"Your first time here?" the female bartender asked me.

My shoulders sagged. "Is it that obvious?"

"Yeah, kinda."

"Can I get a glass of champagne?" I asked.

"What have you seen so far?" she asked as she filled a champagne flute to the brim with Moet.

"I think a better question is, what haven't I seen?"

She smirked. "Yeah, that about describes it. You just gotta find your right level of kink, and you'll feel right at home here."

"Have you ever…partaken in anything here, or do you just serve liquid courage all night?"

"Trust me, most of us don't need the liquid courage to do anything you see goin' on between these walls."

"So, you have?"

She winked at me. "Ain't nothin' wrong with raising a little hell every now and then."

Before I had the chance to respond, Rio appeared beside me. "What's your fantasy, Hermès?" he whispered.

My head suddenly started to buzz a little as I could feel the alcohol finally kicking in. "If I say it, it's gonna sound crazy, stupid or both."

"Tell me…just let that shit fall off your tongue."

I lazily shrugged my shoulder. "I don't know, I've always had this fantasy like meeting a stranger and the passion just being so intense between us, he takes me right in the bathroom or somewhere private where it's just me and him, and fucks me hard, and I let him. I don't fight. I don't scream. I just...give him all of me."

"You want that nigga to talk to you dirty?" he asked, letting his bottom lip gently touch my neck.

The vibrations of his deep voice against my eardrum sent shivers through my body

"I do..."

"How dirty do you want it?"

I could feel the heat reddening my skin. "As dirty as he can get..."

Rio licked his lips. "You sure you can handle that?"

"Yeah."

"Where you want that nigga to touch you?" he asked, skating his fingertips across my lower back, connecting all the erotic dots in my body.

"Everywhere..."

"How hard you want him to fuck you?"

"Real hard."

"Do you want him to make you beg for it?" he asked, running the back of his hand against my arm, instantly creating prickling goosebumps.

"Only for a little bit."

"Mmm, and what you want that nigga's name to be?"

I stared straight into his pools of brown eyes. "Rio," I whispered.

His lips parted. "Good."

I turned to face him fully, and he disappeared. He'd turned my knees to water and vanished. Although he was gone, I still felt breathless, as if he was still breathing down my neck. I was so blindsided by lust my body damn near begged for his touch. I felt raw and open without him. He'd coerced me into opening up and left me open. After thirty minutes of sitting at the bar waiting for him, I decided to pick up my pride and head home. The second I stood to my aching feet, Rio walked up to me.

"Don't tell me you're leaving," he said.

"Yeah, I am. I've had enough for one night."

"And I was just about to muster enough courage to ask if I could buy you a drink."

"No, thank you. I'm good."

"Hold up a sec," he said, gently grabbing my arm.

I looked down at his hand and then back up at him. "What?"

"Take a shot of Henny with me first."

"I don't need any harder liquor in my system. I gotta drive home."

"C'mon, it's just one shot. It'll put some hair on your chest."

"Why in the fuck would I want that?" I asked, frowning at him.

"Oh, there she is. She's getting feisty," he joked.

"Shut up."

"I'll shut up if you take this shot with me, then I'll bid you good-night. Deal?"

I chewed my bottom lip and then sat back down. "Fine. One shot."

"My name is Rio, by the way," he said, extending his hand to me as if it were our first meeting.

I looked down at his hand and then darted my eyes up to his. He was wearing a smirk while biting on his bottom lip. He was portraying my fantasy right in front of my eyes.

"What happens here stays here," he whispered to me.

I sat back at the bar and let him order us a round of shots. By the time I stood up from the bar, I was stumbling. Rio hooked his strong arm around my waist and walked me to the stairs.

"Oh my God, I cannot believe I went shot for shot with you! I don't even drink!" I whined.

"I can tell," he chuckled.

I leaned against the railing, and he put his hand above my head and towered over me. "You know you're beautiful, right? Don't ever let any man make you feel any different," he said, pressing his lips against my nape.

"You really think so?" I asked, cocking my neck to the side.

"You're the most beautiful woman I've ever seen. If you were mine, I'd show you how much I loved you every night," he said, swiping my curls behind my ear.

"What if I could be?"

He took a step back from me. "Don't tempt me, Hermès. Whether you acknowledge it or not, you're already taken."

"What if I'm ready to change it?"

"Don't waste that change on me."

"What do I have to lose? You can't break a heart that's already broken, Rio."

He shook his head. "A nigga like me will still find a way."

"Feel that?" I asked, putting his large hand on my chest.

"Yeah."

"That's what a broken heart beats like...I know you're no good for me. You think I don't? I'm not talkin' about my heart tonight, Rio. You say you a freak, right? Show me what's in your bag of tricks."

"Wait for me upstairs."

"What room?"

His lips brushed past my ear, making the hair on my neck rise. "Seven."

"Seven," I repeated.

I walked upstairs with a pounding heart. I could feel him staring a hole in my back, but I refused to turn around. I stood in front of door number seven and grabbed the handle. The second I twisted the knob, Rio spun me around and pressed my back against the door.

"I made it..."

He cut me off by placing his lips on mine. He kissed me like I hadn't been kissed in years. His lips were warm and full, and I could feel myself melting under his herculean frame. He scooped me into his arms, making me feel as weightless as a feather, and carried me to the canopy bed. He laid me on top of the silk red sheets amongst the red rose petals on top.

"Rio..."

"You said you wanted me to show you, right? Hold on tight, baby girl."

His large hands glided up my thigh and parted the wetness between them. "Damn, Hermès...you want this, don't you?" he asked, his voice husky and deep.

I shifted my bottom lip between my teeth and nodded hesitantly. "I do."

"Go on, touch it. You can have whatever you want tonight. Your beautiful ass deserves it," he said, placing my hand on the bulge in his pants.

"Mmm, shit," I whispered.

The more my hand rubbed against the imprint in his jeans, the more I could feel myself giving into my inhibitions.

"I shouldn't, we shouldn't," I groaned between kisses.

"We grown. That means we can do whatever the fuck we want."

"I'm trying really hard to contain myself right now. This is me fighting the apple," I confessed.

"Don't fight it, Hermès. Bite that shit. Better yet, come here and ride that shit," he said, flipping me onto his lap. I slid my clammy hands up the inside of his shirt and started digging my nails into his hard shell of a chest as he lifted my dress above my waistline. Rio pushed my panties to the side and shoved two fingers inside my sweet spot. I moaned in his mouth as he pushed his fingers deeper inside me while flicking my throbbing clit with his thumb. The louder my moans became, the harder I could feel his dick getting as it pressed against my inner thigh.

With my eyes slammed shut, I listened to him whisper the words *'Tell me you want it'* repeatedly in my ear as his fingertips coursed down my spine. I slowly pulled my mouth away. His words were fogging my brain as I panted uncontrollably. Each sweet kiss disarmed me until I became putty in his arms. There was no doubt in my mind that I wanted him.

"There are rules, Rio," I breathed while grinding against his fingers.

"Fuck the rules. I'll break all of them mothafuckas for you," he grumbled.

Rio's tongue swirled around mine as I ran my hands freely down his face. He slowly pulled away and ran his thumb down my lips before kissing me again. Before I knew it, Rio had placed me back on my back. My heart fluttered as he kissed down my stomach while never losing eye contact with me. He lowered himself between my thighs and placed my hand on top of my flower. He licked my fingers while I rubbed my clit through my dripping wet, red lace panties. His soft lips left a trail of sloppy, wet kisses on my inner thighs before sliding off my panties. Rio continued to lick my fingertips until I slowly slid my hand up and felt his tongue against my warm, wet skin. My toes curled as I threw my head back in ecstasy. No inhibitions or ring would stop me.

"Ooooh shiiiiiiiitttttttt!" I screamed out in pleasure.

With my head tilted toward the ceiling, I opened my eyes to see ropes and chains hanging from the top of the bed and a shelf filled with whips, paddles, and handcuffs across the room. I closed my eyes and ran my hands over his head full of waves. He tongue kissed my pussy with such precision I didn't know what to do. My body jerked and flinched as he snaked his tongue in and out of me.

"That feels so good. Mmm, shit. Just like that," I moaned.

"Don't stop?" he asked.

"Mmm, no, don't stop. Make me cum, Rio."

"Give me every last drop of it, baby girl."

I bucked my hips forward while running my feet down his perfectly sculpted back muscles. Rio was different. He was a man burning to learn my truth and my body to make me whole again.

"Take your shirt off," I told him.

Rio flashed his eyes up at me from in between my thighs and reached behind his head to pull his shirt off with one hand while finger fucking me with the other.

"Mmm, shit."

"Take your clothes off. I just wanna look at your body. It's fucking amazing," he said as he stepped back to drop his pants and stroke his dick.

I dropped the straps of my dress off my shoulder and slid it down around my ankles before stepping out. I lowered my gaze to his chocolate eggplant, and my mouth began to water. I flipped my hair to the side before kissing down his abs. The closer I got to his dick, the more it pulsated inside his boxers.

"Mmm, tell me how bad you want this dick," he mumbled.

I licked my lips while batting my long faux eyelashes up at him. "I want it so bad."

Rio pulled my body to his while staring at me in awe. He spread my legs wide and pulled me onto his dick.

"Ooooh fuck!" I screamed while tugging on my nipples.

He locked his arms underneath my legs and pumped into me with no mercy. Rio pulled my hair and smacked my ass until I came not once, not twice, but three times before he'd even cum once. He pulled out of me and walked around the bed to grab a bottle of oil, a feather, and satin wrist ties.

My eyes widened. "What's all that for?"

"Don't be scared. You don't know what you like until you try it."

He climbed on top of me, grabbed my wrists, and tied the black satin ties around them. Once it was secure, he palmed some warm oil to my skin and massaged it all over my body. I was completely relaxed. The feather sent shivers racing through my body as it swiped against my spine.

"Tell me how you feel right now."

"I feel good. I feel *really* good," I told him.

"Do you remember my safe word?"

"Ecstasy," I repeated to him.

"Yeah, remember to say it only if you need it, and remember just to relax."

My teeth sunk into my bottom lip when his face disappeared in between my thighs again. With my wrists tied, I pulled myself up and hooked my wrists behind his head while thrusting my pussy against his lips.

"Mmm, shit. Don't stop. Right—right there," I ached out.

Just before I came, he flipped me on top of him and slammed me down onto his hard-ass dick. I started riding him as hard as I could. I bucked against him, not caring about how loud I was or how I looked. My glossy chest bounced against his as I locked my nails into his muscular shoulders.

"Oh, you want this bad, don't you?" he asked.

"Mmhm," I moaned.

He smacked my ass as I rode him. I watched him rub on my nipples while I bounced on top of his dick like a pogo stick. Our breathing was heavy and rugged as he palmed my ass and bounced it up and down against him.

"Fuckkkkkkkk! I'm about to cum!" I screamed.

"Mmm, save that cum for me until I tell you to squirt all over this dick," he groaned as he thrust into me.

Rio slid out of me and untied my wrists so that I could crawl off the bed. He walked me into the corner of the room where there was a leather sex swing suspended in the air by chains. He swooped me into his arms and sat me inside. I wrapped my hands around the chains as Rio stepped in between my legs and held my ankles. He lifted my legs over his shoulders and buried his tongue deep inside me while clawing at my lower back.

"Ooooh, my God! Yessss! Yessss! Fuck!" I moaned.

Rio ran his fingertips down my waist while he watched as my hair-less flower slid onto his dick with ease. My breasts bounced freely, jiggling to the cadence of his merciless, deep strokes. While inside the swing, Rio continued twisting my body like a pretzel at his command. He wrapped my legs around his neck like a medal of honor as he thrust deep into me at an angle.

"Mmm, fuck! Deeper, baby! Deeper!"

"You ready to cum for me, baby girl?" he asked.

"Yessss! I'm gonna cum.!"

"Where you gon' cum, baby girl? You gon' cum all on this dick?"

"Fuck yessss!" I screamed as my body tingled in ecstasy.

I spent stolen hours intertwining my body with his. By the time we were done, I felt like I'd just finished running two miles at full speed. Our night together was something I'd never forget.

## CHAPTER 8

# Never Gonna Say Goodbye

**Hermès**

Fucking Rio brought something out of me that I hadn't felt in a very long time. It was the best sex I'd ever had. I lay entangled in the sheets, feeling like a brand-new woman. My makeup was smeared across the pillows and sheets like an artistic masterpiece. I'd come home and passed out without washing Rio's scent. Being with him was the first time in a long time that I felt seen by anything other than my own reflection. I slowly ran my fingertips over my lips and closed my eyes. I could still feel Rio's hands on my body, taking control. I snapped out of my daze when I heard the bedroom door open. I quickly turned on the sink to let the water run. Cap stepped inside before I could get over to the door to lock it. He sat on top of the toilet and looked at me.

"I'm ready to talk."

I screwed up my face. "Talk? You wanna talk after you practically pimped me out!"

"I'm sorry about that. I'm sorry about all of it, okay? I want to talk about you and me."

I rolled my eyes. "What about us, Cap?"

"I love you, baby."

"Cap, please stop."

"No, I want you to listen to me, all right? I'm just as mad at myself as you are. I fucked up," he said as he pounded his chest like a barbarian.

His half-ass apology did nothing but catapult me straight back into the sad reality of my life. He was eight hours too late. Neither my heart nor my thighs were open for business any longer.

"And to show you how sorry I am, I got you somethin'," he said, reaching out for my hands.

I folded my arms across my chest, afraid to get too close to him, not knowing if I still smelled like Rio. "What is it?"

"Go outside and see."

We walked downstairs and over to the front door as I swung it open. Cap dug in his pocket and pressed the button. The bright LED headlights on a white Rolls Royce truck lit up.

"What's this?"

"It's yours, baby. I wanted to show you how sorry I am."

I scoffed. "Wow."

"You don't like it?"

"What the fuck are you even still doing here, Cap? Don't you got a new bitch with a baby to take care of?"

"All you ever do is disrespect me. You want shit to change and go back to the way it used to be all because the truth has hunted you down?"

"Listen, I know I made a mess out of all this shit. I'm just asking you for a chance to fix this. I still love you, Hermès. All I need you to do is tell me that you love me. I made a choice, and I'm sticking to it. I promise you, I've learned my lesson," he said before grabbing my waist and kissing me.

Cap's lips left mine, and he took a few steps back, leaning against the closet door in the foyer. It was nothing like the kiss I'd shared with Rio. It lacked passion. "You really not fuckin' with me, baby?"

I stared at him with a blank look on my face. Truth was, I didn't know what to say. I was at a toss-up. A part of me knew my kids deserved to grow up in a household where they saw their mother and father daily. The other part knew my girls, and I deserved better than Cap. He was selfish, and he didn't deserve their love.

"I just need time, Cap."

"Time for what?"

"To think about what I want. You had your time, didn't you? Give me mine."

"How much time do you need?" he asked.

"I'll let you know when I'm ready," I said, walking past him to ascend the stairs.

* * *

## Rio

"The shipment will arrive tonight," I mumbled as I read Vez's text message out loud. Before I could acknowledge his message, my phone started to ring.

"Yo, hello?" I answered.

"I've got good news," Cap said to me.

"Word? I'm always in the mood for some good news. What's up?"

"Nothin' is official yet, but I talked to my connect over at the district attorney's office, and it looks like everything is going to be dropped."

"That ain't good news, that's great news, nigga. You said you'd come through, and you did."

"I told you, I'm a man of my word. So, once this all goes away, don't forget what you owe me," Cap reminded me.

"I got you. Don't you worry about that."

"So, what will you do to celebrate the good news?"

I huffed. "Shit, to tell you the truth, I hadn't thought about it."

"All that pussy you get thrown at you daily, and you ain't thought about which one you wanna sample?"

"Nah, I never believe the hype," I told him.

"Shit, that couldn't be me."

"Are you forgetting I've seen your wife? You better act like you know what you got before it's gone."

"What I tell you about mentioning my wife? I suggest you mind your business, all right?"

"Say less, nigga. I'm just tryna look out for you and let you know that if you stray away from home too long, there's gon' be another nigga fuckin' her better than you ever did. Is that what you want?"

"What the fuck did I just say?" Cap growled. "Shit is good in my house, all right? You worry about the shit you got goin' on, and you let me worry about who the fuck my wife is fuckin' and who she ain't."

I let out a howl of a laugh. "Yo, chill. Why so serious, nigga? I was just jokin' with yo uptight ass."

Cap exhaled into the phone. "Yeah, all right. Just remember what I said."

I ended the call and dialed Vez's number to tell him the good news. "Yo, what up?" I asked him when he answered the phone.

"What up, nigga? You get my text?"

"Yeah, and I got news for you, nigga."

"Good or bad?"

"Great. My lawyer got the charges against me dropped. A nigga is gettin' off clean."

"Word? That's what's up. Does this mean what I think it means?"

I nodded. "Hell yeah."

Getting off meant we could go after Carlo for having diarrhea of the mouth. He was going to have to suffer the consequences for even whispering my name anywhere near the feds. I had a reputation to uphold not only in the business world but in the streets, too. I would have to make an example out of Carlo, no matter who he was to me.

\* \* \*

Later that night, I was in the club with a drink in my hand when I saw Hermès walk in wearing a black dress that hugged her body in all the right places and a pair of blackout sunglasses. I waited until she found a seat at the bar and ordered a drink before walking over to her.

"Back for more already?" I asked while leaning against the empty bar stool beside her.

She shot me a lazy grin while shaking her head. "Not exactly."

"Did you come here to congratulate me?"

"On what?"

"Cap didn't tell you? He's getting the charges dropped against me."

Her eyes widened. "Wow? That's good—no, that's great news. Congratulations."

"I would appreciate that a lot more if you took off your sunglasses. You're drawing more attention to yourself with them than you realize."

"Why? I can see you just fine."

"I want to look in your eyes when I talk to you, that's why."

She slowly slid the glasses off her face. "Speaking of talk...is there somewhere we can do that privately? Like your office or something?"

I chewed the inside of my jaw for a few seconds while watching her body language. She kept her eyes focused on her drink whenever she spoke to me, as if she was scared or nervous. "Yeah, follow me."

She stood to her feet and noticed the gun on my hip. "What's that about?"

"What's what about?"

"Your gun," she pointed.

"It's just for protection."

"Protection from what or who?"

"Just protection, that's all. Now, c'mon."

I led us through the sea of partygoers until we got behind my closed office doors.

"He wants to work on our marriage...," she blurted out.

My jaw clenched and then went back to normal. "And what do you want, Hermès? Because what you want is all I give a fuck about."

"I don't know...all I know is I won't be able to figure it out until my head is clear, which means...cutting ties with all of my distractions."

"I'm a distraction to you?"

"I didn't mean it like that...It was just a meaningless one-night stand to you, right?"

I cut my eyes at her. "I'll holla at you."

"Wait, what? Stop. Don't walk away from me. I'm sorry if I

offended you. I—I just thought that you had your fill every night at *The Vault.* Why do you care if you lose me?"

"Nah, you don't get to turn this shit around on me."

"Excuse me? What am I turning around on you? I'm just simply stating the facts, Rio."

"That's false as fuck. You talkin' about what you think you know, but that's exactly where your ass went wrong. You're scared of me and everything that I represent."

"And what's that?"

"Freedom. The choice to be whoever the fuck you want, whenever you want. You crave that shit. I can see it in your eyes."

"You don't know shit about me or what I want, so I suggest you just leave shit where it was—in *The Vault* because what happened that night can never happen again."

I closed the space between us and wrapped my arms around her waist. "You remember the way I had your ass clenching the sheets and climbin' the walls for hours? You sure you wanna give all that up?" I asked, caressing the side of her cheek.

She quickly grabbed my hand and stepped back. "Please don't make this harder than it needs to be..."

"Is this what you want?"

She pushed the air out of her cheeks. "I—I don't know. I just know that if I don't cut this off now, there's a good chance that I'll probably lose everything I've got."

"When are you gon' stop runnin' scared?"

"Stop saying I'm scared, Rio! I'm not fuckin' scared! I just—I have a lot to fuckin' think about, okay? And right now, I just need to distance myself from you as much as possible. It's what's best for everybody."

"You only speakin' for yourself."

She huffed. "I'm sorry things couldn't be different. I—I'm just sorry, okay? Goodbye, Rio."

I watched her storm out of my office and looked up when I saw Vez standing in the doorframe. Her pussy was better than any other woman I'd ever been with. It was a shame she was going to have to learn the hard way when it came to dealin' with niggas like the one she was married to. Nothing she ever did would be enough for him. She'd always try to keep up with him while he searched for the next big thing.

"You good, nigga?" Vez asked me while patting my shoulder.

I snapped out of my trance, turned my glass to my lips, and nodded. "Everything good. You got your piece on you?"

"Never leave the crib without it."

"Good. Let's go get at that nigga, Carlo."

* * *

## Cap

When I got off the phone with Rio, the official word came through that the charges against him would be dropped within twenty-four hours. The second I got my cut from what he owed me plus the drugs he was running through *the Vault*, I was done doin' business with his ass. He may have been respected in the streets, but I'd gotten so many street niggas off the hook in court I had just as much as he did.

Instead of calling him back, I called Carlo. Little did people know I'd also represented him a few times for some of his minor hiccups with the judicial system. The last time we worked together, he told me about the payday that could be in store for me by working with Rio and *The Vault.*, if I introduced him to one of my former clients, a big drug connect.

"What up?" Carlo answered.

"Everything is good my way, you?"

"Everything Gucci."

"I got the charges dropped against your boy."

"That nigga is no longer my nigga, all right? I don't give a fuck if we got the same warm blood runnin' through our veins. All I see is dollar signs, nigga. Fuck all that other shit."

"Whoever he is to you, I got his ass off, and I'm done with him. I don't like the way the mothafucka talks to me."

"Just play it cool, all right? You ain't gon' have to deal with his ass much longer."

"Yeah, whatever. I'm sick of this nigga."

We were in business together once I put Carlo and Rio in touch with the connect I represented a few years back. A few months in, Carlo devised the plan to get Rio out of the way for good so that we'd only have to worry about splitting the money between us after giving the connect his cut. He told me that Rio kept a stash of cash and drugs in his home, so I called in the anonymous tip to one of my friends at the DEA. All we had to do was sit back and wait for the feds to do their job. Everything was good until Rio asked me to represent him and get him off the exact charges I tried to make him go down for. I couldn't say no when he showed me he had the dollars and the sense to back it all up.

"Shit, you just helped that nigga beat a case? He can't do shit else but trust you, nigga."

"Yeah, he definitely trusts me."

"Good, so does that mean you're ready to move on to the next phase of the plan? If so, I'll drop the bug in my guy's ear to do what we discussed."

"Yeah, but just wait until I get my money, and then you can move on that nigga however you see fit. Just make sure you keep it clean, all right? You do it right, and I promise you, you'll be livin' off what I give you for a long time..."

## CHAPTER 9

# The Heir to the Throne

## Hermès

I stood in the middle of the girl's bedroom with a laundry basket full of freshly washed clothes to put away. Books, stuffed animals, dolls, and dress-up clothes were scattered all over the floor. After placing the basket down on Melody's brightly colored bedspread, I walked over to open her white dresser drawer.

"Ouch! Fuck!" I yelled out and grabbed my foot.

I looked down and realized I'd stepped on one of her Barbie doll's shoes. I quickly swiped the bottom of my foot and saw a little bit of blood on my hand.

"What's wrong?" Cap asked, standing in the doorway.

I turned my neck towards him. "What? N—nothing's wrong. I—I just stepped on one of the girls' damn toys."

"Are you bleeding?"

"A little bit. I'm trying not to get it on the carpet," I told him while balancing my weight on one foot.

"Here, let me help you," he said as he approached me.

Cap scooped me into his arms and carried me out of their bedroom and into our master bathroom. He set me next to the sink while he ran cold water onto a torn paper towel and pressed it to the bottom of my foot.

"Better?"

I nodded. "Y—yeah, um, thank you."

"Where do you keep the band-aids? I haven't hurt myself in forever. I don't even know where they are."

"Bottom drawer to the left," I told him.

Cap found a band-aid and placed it on the bottom of my foot. "There you go, all brand new."

I smiled without showing any teeth. "Thank you...I keep telling the girls they need to pick up after themselves when they—"

He cut me off with an unexpected kiss. It was long and unwarranted, but I didn't have it in me to stop him. If we were going to remain husband and wife, I had to be able to give him my all. As soon as the kiss ended, silence took over the room.

"Uh, damn," he said before letting out a soft chuckle.

I belted out a nervous chuckle alongside him as if we were just a couple of teenagers who didn't know the first thing about making out.

"I'm sorry if that was—"

"No, it was fine," I said, cutting him off.

Cap looked into my eyes while brushing some of my hair out of my face. "I'm sorry...for everything."

I nodded. "I know...me too."

"What do you have to be sorry for?"

I shrugged one shoulder. "For letting my emotions get the best of me...for everything."

Cap smiled before pulling his lips onto mine again. He rested both hands around my neck while kissing me deeper. The longer we kissed, the more I could feel the spark returning.

"Mmm, I missed this," he growled against my lips.

"Me too," I breathed.

He pulled me to the edge of the countertop while pulling down his sweatpants. With my panties pushed to the side, he broke past my walls and filled me up with every inch of him.

"Mmm, shit. I'm sorry, baby. I'm so sorry," he whispered while nibbling on my neck. "Tell me you forgive me, baby."

I nodded. "I do—I forgive you," I moaned.

"Tell me this pussy is mine."

"It's yours, Cap."

"Til' death do us part?"

"Yes, baby. Til' death do us part."

Just as he began to pick up the pace, his phone vibrated against the nightstand in the bedroom.

"Ignore it, baby," I panted.

"I am," he said, thrusting as deep as he could.

The phone stopped vibrating, only to start up again a minute later. I felt him start to pull away and tightened my grip around his neck. "Please don't stop, Cap. I need you," I begged him.

"It might be work, baby. I—I gotta answer it."

Cap pulled out of me, pulled his pants up, and darted out of my sight. After waiting three minutes, I climbed off the countertop and entered the bedroom.

"Is everything okay?" I asked, caressing his back and shoulders from behind.

He turned to look at me with a distressed look in his eyes. "I'm sorry, but I gotta go."

"What's wrong? Did something happen at work?"

"No."

"Then what is it?"

"It's Tia...she went into labor early. I—I gotta get to the hospital."

I frowned. "What?"

"I'm sorry."

"I swear to God if you leave, I nor the kids will be here when you decide to bring your ass back!" I yelled.

"This is my child too, Hermès. I gotta be there."

"Do what the fuck you gotta do, just remember what I said."

I stood back and watched him throw a shirt on, grab his wallet and keys, and head out of the bedroom door.

* * *

## Cap

The second I slammed my body into my car, I sped to the hospital to be by Tia's side. I had every intention of stopping by her house in the coming weeks to tell her I'd decided to stay with Hermès, but going into labor early threw a curveball into my plans.

By the time I'd gotten into the delivery room, Tia was already pushing our son out. I raced to her side and held her hand.

"That's it, Tia! You can do it. Give me two more big pushes so you can bring your son into the world," the doctor told her.

"Ahhhhhhhh!" she screamed out.

"Perfect! One more push, and you can say hello to your son. Give me one more in three, two, one, push!" the doctor coached.

"You got this baby! Bring our son into the world," I told her as she looked into my eyes.

Her eyes were tired but still had a fire in them. That was enough to tell me that she had it under control. She pressed her chin into her chest and slammed her eyes shut as she pushed. Seconds later, we all heard the melodious cries of my firstborn son.

"Here he is," the nurse said, placing him in Tia's arms.

"He's beautiful, Cap. He looks just like you."

I looked down at her and smiled. "He does. Welcome to the world, Julius Jr."

* * *

Three hours later, Tia had been cleaned up and was resting in her bed while I held our son. There were thousands of emotions running through my head at once. As much as I wanted to be in the same house as my son day in and day out, I knew there was no way Hermès or Tia would go for having half of me any longer. I looked into my son's eyes and knew there would be hard decisions I would have to make.

"Baby?" Tia asked as she rubbed her eyes.

"We're right here," I told her.

"Let me hold him."

I waited until she sat upright in the bed before handing the baby to her. She stared into his sleeping face and gently ran her finger over his head of dark hair before securing his hat.

"Thank you," I told her.

"For what, bae?"

"Giving me my son."

"It was meant to be, just like you and I."

I gave her a half smile. "You know, I always wanted a son. No offense to my daughters because I love them but having him completes me. I know I wouldn't have him if I never met you."

Tia smiled. "Aww, I love you too, baby."

I swallowed hard. "I'm going to stay with her, Tia."

She slowly dragged her eyes away from the baby's face and looked up at me. "You don't mean that."

I nodded. "I do."

"No, you're just confused right now, that's all."

"I was confused for a long time, and I've been doin' a lot of thinkin...I have to keep my family together, Tia."

"What about us, huh? Aren't we your family, too?"

"Of course you are. That's not what I meant."

"We're just the family you'll make time for on President's Day or Labor Day, right? My son will never know what it feels like to see his father on the holidays that fuckin' matter, like Christmas or Easter."

"That's not true, and you know it. I already told you my son will have everything he needs and more."

"Everything except for a fuckin' full-time father, right? Why does my son gotta miss out on that shit just because you wanna go pretend to be super dad underneath a different roof?"

"Tia—"

"I gave you everything I had, Cap! I trusted you with everything! Now you tell me you're done? Just like that? What about me, huh? What about my fuckin' feelings? I'm sitting in a fuckin' hospital bed, nigga! I just had your baby! Your firstborn son! Your wife could never do that shit for you!" she yelled.

"Yo, calm down with the yellin' while you got my son in your arms."

"Don't act like you give a fuck now. The moment you leave here, you'll go back to your house on the hill with your perfect wife and kids while we do what? Take your hush money every month to stay in the shadows?"

I shook my head. I knew first-hand what it felt like to grow up in a house without my father. As much as I said it didn't affect me, I knew it did. The last thing I wanted to do was put my seed through that.

"Just let me figure some shit out, all right? I'm gon' work it out for everybody."

"Work it out how Cap? Huh?"

I shrugged as the wheels in my head started turning. "You and the baby can come move in with us."

Her eyes widened. "That's bullshit, and you know it. The moment Hermès sees me coming, she will try to smother me in my sleep."

"You don't have to worry about her. I got her."

She scoffed. "Yeah, I'm sure you do."

"I meant what I said, all right? Just give me some time to work out all the logistics, and I promise you that you, me, and our son will all be under the same roof when you leave this hospital."

"Do you promise?"

I walked over and kissed her forehead and then leaned down to kiss my son. "I promise."

* * *

I walked through the door the following day to see Hermès in the kitchen cooking the girls chocolate chip pancakes while they sat in the living room watching "SpongeBob SquarePants."

"Daddy! Daddy!" Melody squealed.

"Hey, baby girl," I said, pulling her into my arms.

I walked into the kitchen and looked at Hermès. "Good morning."

Instead of speaking to me, she turned her attention to the girls. "Girls, breakfast is ready!"

"Daddy, guess what?" Symphony asked.

"What?"

"Grandma Grace is coming to get us today!"

I shot my eyes over to Hermès. "Oh really? Why is Grandma Grace coming all the way here?"

"I'm sending the girls to my mother's house for a week so you and I can figure things out," Hermès answered.

I nodded. "I think that's a good idea because there are some things we need to discuss."

"Things like what?" she asked.

"Girls, why don't you take your pancakes into the living room and sit on the floor in front of the TV so you can finish watching Sponge-Bob, okay?" I told them.

"Yay, SpongeBob!" Melody cheered.

Once they were out of earshot, I walked over to Hermès and leaned against the kitchen counter while she piled a couple of dishes into the dishwasher.

"Hermès, look at me."

"I can hear you just fine."

I grabbed her by her waist, and she swatted my hand away. "Don't you dare touch me."

I sighed. "Look, I know shit is fucked up, but I have a responsibility to my son, okay? I need to be there for him."

"Then go do that under that bitch's roof."

I looked down at the floor and then back up at her. "Her roof is our roof."

She creased her forehead. "What?"

"I told her that she and the baby could come to stay with us when she got out of the hospital."

"You did what?" she yelled.

"In the guest house. That way, I can be there for my son, and it doesn't have to be under two different roofs. He'll also get to know his sisters and vice versa."

"You just got it all figured out, don't you? Your wife and your mistress under the same roof sounds pretty badass to me, huh Cap? Are you out of your mothafuckin mind? I will NOT put up with that shit! Do you hear me? It's us or them, Cap!"

"What the fuck do you want me to do, Hermès, huh? He's MY son!"

"What do I want you to do? I want you to keep your fuckin' dick in your pants! I want you to not cheat on me with God knows who! I want you not to have a membership at a fuckin' sex club behind my back!"

My eyes widened. "H—hold up. What sex club? How the fuck did you find out about that?"

"It doesn't matter how I found out, okay? Just fuckin' know that I know! God, Cap—you don't give a fuck about me! I can't believe I bought into all that shit about you being sorry and you wanting this to work!"

"I meant everything I said, Hermès! I do love you, and I do love the girls, too. I also have another kid that I need to be there for, and this is the best way I know how to do it. Please, just consider him. He's a baby, Hermès. He will need his father more than ever in the world that we live in now. I can't be to him what my father was to me. I can't fuckin' do that shit!"

She huffed while folding her arms across her chest. "And what do I tell the girls when they see you holding a new baby that they knew nothing about, huh?"

"We're going to tell them the truth."

"They are children, Cap! They can't handle the truth! I will not let you put the burden of your mistake on their shoulders! I won't!"

"I just want my family together, baby. That's all I want."

"Well, moving in your mistress and your bastard is the only sure way you'll rip your family apart," she spat.

I could feel the blood boiling under my skin. I understood she was hurt and had every right to be, but I was still the man of the house, the breadwinner, and the shot-caller. If she couldn't fall in line with what I wanted, she could pack her bags, and I'd raise the girls and my son under the same roof without her.

"Look, I tried to be nice about this shit because I understand what I did to you. A broken heart don't heal overnight, but this is my house, Hermès. Who paid for the clothes on your back? Mine. If I want my son under the same roof as me, that's what's going to happen. This shit ain't up for discussion no more."

## CHAPTER 10

*Triggered*

**Hermès**

I stormed out of the kitchen in a huff and didn't stop until I was locked behind the bedroom door alone. My hands were shaking uncontrollably as I tried to settle my jagged breathing. I was an emotional wreck who was seconds away from having a full-blown panic attack.

"I'm so stupid! I'm so fucking stupid!" I yelled while smacking my forehead with the palm of my hand.

I couldn't believe I'd let him in again so easily for him to run the second he got a call from his mistress, let alone tell me he would move her into our home. It was one thing to do his dirt in the darkness, but to flaunt his indiscretions in my face day after day was cruel. I wasn't shit to him. He didn't give a fuck about me or our children. All he cared about was himself and what he wanted. It was time to focus on what and who was best for me.

Once my mother had picked up the kids, I knew it was game time. If he wanted to play with my heart and pull my strings as if he were my puppet master, I would show him what it was like to get played. After showering and putting on my favorite perfume, I grabbed my purse and keys.

"Where you goin'?" Cap asked while sitting on the couch.

"Out," I said before slamming the door behind me.

My hands began to sweat as I gripped the steering wheel tighter. I'd pulled up in front of Rio's club, seeking refuge from my broken home. I put the truck in park and walked up to the entrance. I pulled on the door and noticed it was locked. My eyes darted down to my watch. It was the middle of the day, which was too early for anyone to be inside a nightclub. Feeling like I'd gotten the air let out of my balloon, I turned to head back to my car.

"Hermès?"

I quickly turned around to see Rio standing in the doorway. "H—hey. I didn't mean to disturb you. I didn't realize it was too early for your club to be open."

"What are you doing here?"

My breath hitched. "I—I don't know."

"You do know."

I sighed. "I just—I don't know how to say I was wrong."

"You just did."

"You were right about everything...I was scared. I still am."

"And?" he asked.

"And...I would really like to come in."

"Come in for what?"

"Um, t—to talk."

"We ain't got shit to talk about. You made yourself clear the last time I saw you. So, if you don't mind, I got shit to handle," he said before closing the door.

"Rio, please. I—I need you. I need what you bring out of me. I'm so lost right now. My world is completely upside down, and you were the first thing to come in and make me feel like shit was going to be alright again, and I know I screwed that up. This is me apologizing to you and asking you for another chance."

"Another chance to do what? Fuck you again so that you can tell me you don't know what the fuck you want the next day? Nah, I knew you were off limits when I met you, and for some stupid fuckin' reason, I took it there with you anyway, but I'm good now."

"Rio—"

"You know what they say, fool me once, shame on you, but fool me twice, shame on me. I don't give people another chance to fool me again."

I lowered my head in defeat before nodding. "I get it. You're right. I'm a stupid woman. I—I shouldn't have come here. I'll leave you alone."

A car pulled up the second I turned around, and the windows rolled down. Before I had the chance to step off the curb, shots rang out, and everything went black.

* * *

### Three days later.

I woke up to the smell of bleach and day-old hospital food wafting past my nose. The walls were a pale, icy white with fluorescent lighting over my head. For a second, I thought I'd died and gone to Heaven until I saw Cap's sleep-deprived brown eyes staring into mine.

"Oh my God, she's awake! She's finally awake!" he exclaimed.

I looked down at the IV in my arm and the automatic finger clip on my pointer finger. Then, I heard the beeping of the LED heart monitor beside my bed. The corner of the room was filled with get well soon balloons and a colorful bouquet of my favorite flower, tulips. The mixture of smell of the flowers and over-bleached bedding made my stomach churn. Neither was strong enough to cancel out the other.

"W—what happened?" I mumbled.

"You were shot three times," he told me.

My eyes widened. "What?"

"You've had multiple surgeries."

"How long have I been out? Where are the girls?" I asked while trying to move my lower limbs underneath the starchy hospital sheets.

Cap rested his hand on the side railing of my bed. "Three days..."

I was thankful to be alive. The only thing I wanted to do was see my girls' two beautiful faces. "Where are the girls? I want to see the girls."

"Shh, calm down. They are safe. They are with your mother. She wanted to bring them back here, but I told her not to. They don't need to see you like this."

"Like what? What's wrong with me?"

"You're fine, or you will be. You were shot in the stomach, left hand, and your collarbone. They were able to remove all of the fragments from the bullets and stop all the internal bleeding. But..."

"But? But what, Cap?"

"You may not be able to have any more children..."

The air in the room suddenly went thin. It was the last thing I wanted to hear from the last person I wanted to hear it from. I closed my eyes as silent tears slipped out of the corners of my eyes.

"Shh, it's okay, baby. Everything is going to be okay," he told me.

"No, it's not! Nothing is ever going to be okay ever again! Why don't you see that?" I yelled.

"It will be. Everything will be fine as long as you're honest with me."

My forehead creased. "Honest with you about what Cap?" I asked, never even bothering to look up at him.

"Honest about why the fuck were you at Rio's club in the middle of the day in the first place..."

I frowned hard. "What?"

"You heard me, Hermès. Now, tell me the truth. Why the fuck were you at Rio's club in the middle of the day?"

My lips parted, and two words fell out. "My I.D."

His forehead creased. "Your what?"

"You remember the night you *forced* me to go there and give him all that money? After that night, I couldn't find my I.D., so I decided to retrace my steps, starting at the last place I remembered pulling it out, which was there."

Cap eyed me closely. The smug look on his face told me he was still skeptical, but I didn't give a fuck. It was my only excuse, and he would have to take it or leave it. The longer the silence hung between us, the more my thoughts focused entirely on Rio. I know I'd been hit, but had he? Was he in the hospital room next door or the morgue in the basement? Just thinking about never being able to lay my eyes on him again to right my wrongs brought premature tears to my eyes. The second one started to roll down the hills of my cheek, Cap gently wiped it away and kissed my forehead.

"It's okay, baby. I believe you...and we will get through this together. Just you and me."

My eyes rolled way back into my head before I sighed. "So does that mean your whore is staying on the other side of the city where she belongs?" I asked.

His jaw tensed, and then he slowly licked his lips. "Don't you worry about Tia, I got her. All you need to focus on is getting better."

He brushed my hair from my face before leaning in to press his cold lips against mine. It felt like the kiss of death. There was no passion in his icy, wet peck. Before he could say anything, *or worse*, kiss me again, his phone began vibrating in his jacket against the chair. He looked back at it and then over at me.

"Are you going to get that?" I asked.

He looked back at it again and shook his head. "Whoever it is, they can wait."

I looked at him closely for the first time since I'd woken up. He couldn't keep his gaze on a single thing for more than a few seconds before his eyes shifted all over the room. "You can answer it, Cap. It's okay."

He walked over to grab his phone and looked at the screen for a few seconds before facing me. "It's work..."

"It's fine, Cap. Go handle your business."

"I don't think you should be here alone, especially not now that you're awake."

"Who's going to mess with me? There's literally a whole hall full of doctors here."

"Are you sure?"

"Yeah, I honestly want to be alone...to get my thoughts together about what you told me."

"We're going to make it through this together, baby. I promise."

"Where's my phone, Cap? I want to call and talk to the girls. Are they still with my mom?"

"Yeah, she wanted to bring them here to see you, but I didn't think you'd want them to see you like this."

"You're right, I don't. I only want to hear their voices and tell them Mommy is okay."

"Here," he said, placing my cell phone on the table beside my bed.

"Thank you."

"I'll call you later, okay?"

I nodded. "Okay."

Cap walked over and kissed my forehead again before leaving me alone with my thoughts. I slowly reached over to grab the remote to the TV and turned it on when there was a knock on my door. My lips parted to blow hot air out of my cheeks before responding. "Come in."

To my surprise, a nurse walked in carrying a vase filled with a large bouquet of red and white roses. "Mrs. Capone?"

I nodded. "Yes, that's me."

"These just got delivered for you. Where would you like me to put them?"

"Um, you can sit them right here," I said, pointing to the table beside me.

She walked over and slowly placed the large vase down. "These are beautiful."

"Yeah, they are. Thank you."

"Oh look, there's a card. Do you want me to grab it for you?"

"Yes, please."

She grabbed the card and handed it to me. "Your husband loves you."

"What?" I frowned.

"Oh, I just assumed they were from him. I'm sorry."

"No, you're fine. I was just wondering where that came from. You're right, they are from...him."

She smiled. "That's really great. I'll be in with your medication and dinner soon. Until then, just continue to rest."

"Will do."

As soon as she left the room, my head flopped back against the pillow, and a wide smile made its way across my face. Not only was Rio not dead, but he'd sent me flowers with a card that read, *"Get well soon, I'm not through with you yet. 215-780-0001."*

I pressed the card against my chest and started blushing each time I played the words on the card repeatedly in my head. I could hear him whispering it in my ear, so clearly, it was as if he was in the room standing next to me. My heart sank to my feet when my phone started vibrating against the table. I quickly sat up, snapping out of my fantasy, and reached for my phone.

"Hello?" I answered, pressing the speaker button.

"MOMMY!" Both Symphony and Melody squealed into the receiver.

An even wider smile creased my lips. "Oh my God, I miss you both so, so, so, so much! I love you, I love you, I love you!" I squealed.

"We miss you, Mommy. When are we going to come home and see you?" Symphony asked.

I could hear the sadness in her voice. I quickly swiped a tear away and took a deep breath. "You don't worry your pretty little head about that, okay? You'll see me soon!"

"You promise?" Melody asked.

I chuckled. "Yes, baby girl. I promise."

"Okay, girls, give Gramm back the phone so I can talk to your mommy."

"I love you girls! I love you both so much! I promise I'm going to see you soon, okay?"

"We love you, Mommy!" they said in unison before my mom took over the phone again.

"Hello?"

"Yeah, Ma. I'm here."

"How are you feeling today?"

"How'd you even know I was awake?"

"Cap called me not too long ago. He said he was going to handle something for work but wanted to let me know that you'd finally woken up. You know I've been praying for you every second of every day."

I smiled. "Thank you, Ma. I know you have."

"It kills me being unable to be at your side when you need me. Plus, the girls miss you like crazy."

"I miss them both too. Just hearing their voices makes me want to cry."

"They are doing just fine. You don't worry about them. You just worry about getting better so you can come home to them, okay?"

"I know, I am," I said while nodding to assure myself. "Do they have everything they need?"

"They are fine, Hermès. Cap's done a good job bringing them clothes and toys and keeping me posted."

"Oh yeah?" I asked.

"Yeah, every few hours, he'd call with an update. He'd tell me what the doctors said. He'd call every night to check on the girls whenever he couldn't make it down to the house."

"Where do they think I am right now?"

"They think Mommy is on vacation, although Symphony keeps insisting it's your honeymoon." She chuckled. "I don't know where that girl gets off thinking she's grown."

I let out a soft chuckle, followed by a sigh of relief. I was grateful that Cap hadn't made a big deal and scared the girls. I didn't want them to know anything was wrong with me. All I wanted to do was get the hell out of the hospital and get back to them.

"Tell me somethin', baby," my mother said, snapping me back into our conversation.

"What?"

"What were you doing down at some club? When I first found out about the accident, I thought an intruder had broken into your home or something. Then, when Cap told me you'd been a victim of some drive-by at a downtown club, I didn't know what to think."

"Whatever you're thinking, it's not like that," I told her.

"Then what were you doing down there?"

"I'd gone there with a few of Symphony's mom's friends one night for drinks, and after that, I couldn't find my I.D., so while I was out that day, I decided to go by there and see if it was there. The owner told me he'd checked, and it wasn't there, and when I was walking back to my car, well...that's the last thing I remember."

The other line fell silent for a few seconds before I heard my mother sobbing. "I'm just so grateful that you're okay. These girls wouldn't know what to do without you, nor would Cap."

"Why do you keep bringing up Cap as if he's some sort of angel?"

"That's your husband, Hermès, and he's a good man. He's been there by your side through all of this. Why wouldn't I speak highly of my son-in-law? It's not like he's some deadbeat that doesn't take care of you or his girls."

"Because you've always kissed the ground he walks on without seeing the trail of dirt he leaves behind him!" I snapped.

"Excuse me?"

"From the moment you met Cap, he had you licking out of his palm like a kitten with warm milk."

"Hermès, I am going to give your yellow ass a pass because you're probably over there doped up on pain medication, and you don't realize how crazy you're talking to the woman who brought you into this world!"

I sighed while pulling my lips away from the phone. It wasn't her fault. She didn't know the fucked up things her precious son-in-law had put her daughter through. She was just like everybody else who came across Cap, mesmerized and blind to his bullshit. I'll admit I used to be, too. But I'd been given a second chance at life, and I wouldn't waste it loving a man who didn't love me.

"I'm sorry, Ma. I—I just need to lay down. I'm starting to get a headache."

"Okay, I'll call you again in the morning."

"Okay, sounds good. I love you, Ma."

"I love you, too."

There was another knock on the door when I pressed the red button. I didn't know how I was expected to get any "rest" between all the knocks and phone calls I'd been receiving since I opened my eyes. "Come in."

The same nurse who'd brought me the flowers had returned with my dinner and medicine as promised.

"I'm back!"

"Can you just place it over there? I'll get to it in a little bit. I have to make a phone call."

"No problem. I'm sorry, but I must repeat: these flowers are *so* beautiful. I wish I had a man who brought me things like this. You're one lucky woman."

I looked at her, eyeing the roses in admiration. I could see in her eyes that she still hoped to find her true love one day. Who was I to burst her bubble? "Take them, they're yours."

"What?"

"Seriously, take them. They deserve to be with someone who can give them all the water and sunlight they need. I can't do that here in this hospital room. There's barely any real sun shining in through the windows anyway."

"A—are you sure? I truly don't want to impose. They were gifted to you."

"You're not, I promise. I want you to have them."

She walked over, grabbed the heavy glass vase off the table, and turned toward the door. "Thank you so much. This just made my day."

"You're welcome."

As soon as the door closed, I grabbed my phone while holding Rio's card in my other hand. I quickly dialed the number and waited impatiently as it rang. With each ring, my fingers twitched, my eyes jittered, and my teeth clicked until...

"I see you got my flowers," he answered.

"Are you trying to get me killed?" I responded.

"Don't say no shit like that. Not after what happened."

"Too soon, huh?"

"Way too soon."

"Are you okay? I know I'm pretty banged up, but I take it you have to be doing a little better than me to be the one sending flowers."

"I'm aight, healing."

"Where are you?"

"I'm in the crib. Got a sling on my left arm and shit."

My eyes widened. "Are you okay?" I asked.

He chuckled. "Shouldn't I be the one asking you that? I just sent you flowers in the hospital."

I sighed as my mind replayed my earlier conversation with Cap. "I got shot in the hand, the stomach, and the collarbone..."

The phone went silent, and I turned to look at the screen to check my connection. "H—hello?"

"I swear I'm gon' find out who the fuck did this shit, and I'm gon' handle them."

"Rio, it was just one of those things that happens. You may never find out who was behind it."

"Fuck that, don't shit like that happen in front of my club. Niggas already know I don't play that shit. You're crazy if you think those bullets were for you. They were for me, Hermès. You were in the wrong place at the wrong mothafuckin time."

"I—I"

"You don't understand how sorry I am, Hermès. I knew I should've stayed away from your ass the moment I met you."

"Rio, it's not your fault..."

"This is on me, and I know that shit. You just gotta promise that you'll let me make it up to you."

"How?" I asked.

"Any way you want. You just say the word..."

"You do know I'm still legally married, right?"

"You think I give a fuck about a piece of paper?"

"It doesn't sound like it."

"Plus, we both know that pussy is mine now anyway."

All the air in my body left me as a cool tingle snaked down my spine. His words had left me utterly speechless.

"Has your mind changed since our last conversation?" he asked, bringing me back down to earth.

"A lot has changed since the last conversation we had..."

"What does that mean?"

It became a little trickier to breathe all over again. I didn't know what to expect when I called him, but being put on the spot wasn't it.

"And don't say you don't know," he continued.

"What if I don't know, though?"

"What is it that you want, Hermès?"

I sighed. "I just need time."

"How much time?"

"I don't know..."

"Well, when you're ready, you know where to find me."

It took me a few seconds to realize he'd ended the call with that last sentence, yet I was still sitting there with the phone pressed to my right ear. Rio was a stranger. A fuckin' stranger who was into some shit that I had no business getting myself or my children wrapped up in. With pieces of my sanity still intact, I couldn't help but wish I was in his arms again. I couldn't help but take responsibility for the role I played in getting myself laid up in a hospital. No matter how broken, I was the one who'd stepped out on my marriage and foolishly fell for a man who turned my world upside down with one smile: Nario Sullivan.

* * *

## Cap

With my phone grasped tightly in my left hand, I slammed my body into the seat of my Porsche. The guilt I was carrying around had been weighing my shoulders down like boulders ever since I got the call that my wife had been shot. There was no way I could let Hermès find out I was the one who tried to have Rio killed. The bullets she took were all supposed to be for him.

I'd recklessly put the life of the mother of my children at risk. I loved my daughters, but there was no way I could raise them without Hermès. At one point, I planned to groom Tia to be the perfect mother to my son and the ideal stepmother to my daughters, but seeing Hermès laying in that hospital bed, not knowing if she was going to survive, had me thinkin' differently. It had me feelin' different, too.

There was no doubt that Hermès had been through a hell of a few days, but I still wasn't sure if I fully believed her when she told me why she'd been at the club that day. Until there was proof, I was going to let it rock. Besides, I had bigger shit to worry about. Hours after I'd gotten word that Hermès had been shot, I heard that Rio was still breathing. The longer he stuck around, the longer he would have his hand in my money and a vendetta against me and Carlo.

I pulled out my phone and clicked Carlo's name before pushing the speaker phone button. Instead of hearing his voice, the call went straight to voicemail. I hung up and dialed him three more times before leaving a message.

*"You have reached the voicemail box of two-six-seven-five-five-zero-zero-one-three-seven. Please leave a message after the beep."*

**BEEP**

"I don't know what the fuck has got you thinkin' you can't answer your phone all of a sudden, but shit is real serious right now. Call me back, mothafucka."

After ending the call, I decided to dial the number that called me in Hermès' hospital room.

"Cap."

"Tell me you called to give me good news," I said, clenching my jaw.

"Carlo's dead..."

My eyes widened to the size of saucers as my chest palpitated. One-third of the pie was gone. He just wasn't the one I needed it to be. Since Carlo died, Rio would be ready to go to war with me. My life suddenly flashed before my eyes. It was kill or be killed, and I had to think fast.

"We had a deal. You don't stop until the job is done."

"Nah, get it straight, mothafucka. Carlo and I had a deal, not me and you. I followed out what he wanted, and now he's dead," the voice on the other line told me.

The way he said it was more than a simple statement. It was a warning. One that I took heed of within seconds. I was knee-deep in shit, and there was no turning back.

"I'll pay you. You know I'm good for it. Just name your price."

"Three million...cash," he hissed.

I chewed my bottom lip, knowing the nigga was trying to get over, but I needed the extra protection until I could put my game plan into motion. "Fine. Just give me some time."

"Fuck that. You want the protection of me and my hittas. You pay up in twenty-four hours, or you're on your own, nigga. That means you ain't never gon' be safe."

Again, a *warning*. "Keep the line warm. I'll be in touch in twenty-four," I said before the line went dead.

I slammed my fist against the steering wheel while tossing my cell into the passenger seat. *Think, Cap. Use that intelligent ass brain, nigga.*

*We can get out of this. Think.* No one knew I had an offshore account with so much money I'd be set for the rest of my life—me, my kids, and... well, whichever woman in my life had their shit together when it came time to disappear. The voice on the other line was correct. If I didn't come up with some money fast, I would never be safe. If I wasn't safe, my kids weren't safe, and I couldn't have that. It wasn't going to end with me being in a jail cell or a pine box. I was going to end up on top. My fingertips tapped the number to my accountant as I started the engine and shifted the car into drive.

"Jonathan, clear your schedule for the next hour. I need to meet with you right now..."

* * *

### Rio

My left fist was folded so tightly that veins were popping out as my right thumb swept up the cracked screen of Carlo's phone. After Vez put a bullet in the back of his head, he took his phone and brought it to me. It only took two seconds to read the text thread between him and Cap to know they were conspiring against me. Cap ordered the hit on my head, and Carlo, my blood, had been the one to set it all up. It was crazy what money would make niggas do. One minute, you could be thick as thieves with a mothafucka. The next, they were singing like a canary to the feds or slithering against the back of your neck.

The knock on my door was the only thing that tore my eyes away from the screen. I looked up to see Vez coming through my office door. He waited until the door was closed entirely before speaking up.

"Yo, Rio."

"Yeah?"

"I just got word the nigga Cap is payin' some hittas for protection."

"How much?"

"Three mil."

"Tell 'em I'll double it," I told him.

Vez's eyes widened, and I nodded at him, answering his silent question. He knew not to let a question fall past his lips to me. He simply nodded back and exited as quickly as he'd come. I leaned my head against the chair and let out a long breath. The moment my eyes closed, Hermès' face came to mind. I was still fuming inside after what had happened to her. She didn't deserve to take a bullet, especially not ones that were meant for me. She had no idea the coward she'd married and had kids by. Luckily, she had daughters and no sons. If so, they'd be cowards just like their bitch ass daddy. I could smell a bitch nigga a mile away, and that's precisely what he was.

A nigga like that didn't deserve a woman like Hermès. Shit, neither did I. As much as I wanted to save her, I couldn't. Shit had gotten bigger than her, and I didn't want a mothafucka to ever misconstrue my retaliation as being over some pussy. Nah, it was personal. He'd put a hit out on my life, and I would let him think he was safe until it was too late for him to realize that he wasn't.

CHAPTER 11

# Slow Burn

**Hermès**

*Three months later.*

I t had been about three months since I'd gotten shot, and I still hadn't gotten Rio entirely out of my system. Amongst dealing with a broken collarbone and trying to heal all over with the help of my physical therapist, he still managed to creep into my thoughts, mainly at night. During the day, I focused on getting as close to one hundred percent as possible so I could be there for my children the way they needed me to be.

Although I was back in the house, my bed was still cold. Cap spent most of his time tending to his side bitch and their infant son. It wasn't as if I minded. Half the time, I wasn't present in my own body. I felt as if I'd been sleepwalking through life for the past ninety days. Two kids and one failed marriage later. My life had gone drastically off the beaten path. It was like watching my own house burn down slowly. I was lost, swallowed up by life.

My thoughts were interrupted when I heard the doorbell ring. I glanced over at my phone. It was nine o'clock sharp, which meant my physical therapist, Jewel, had arrived just as she had every morning. After our hour session, I stood at the front door waving as she backed out of the long driveway. Once I could no longer see her, I closed the door and headed for the kitchen. The second my foot slid against the marble floor, and my eyes landed on Tia's silhouette, I instantly regretted my decision.

"Why are you in here? The guest house has a full kitchen," I griped at her.

"The microwave is broken, and I need to warm up my son's bottle."

"Tell Cap to fix it." I shrugged.

She sucked her teeth. "I did, and he hasn't."

I rolled my eyes while looking her up and down. I could not do advanced yoga or Pilates during my healing process. Meanwhile, Tia had snapped back so good it looked like she was just the hired babysitter. I hated everything about her. She was a snake in the grass, and I didn't know how Cap could've gotten tangled up with her in the first place. One good look at her, and it was clear she couldn't be trusted. She was one of those bitches that would lie and say she was pregnant just to get money for the abortion and then spend that shit on some red bottoms. She was far from a smart bitch.

Just as I turned to leave with my bottled water in hand, Cap walked in. He smiled at me. "How you feelin'?" he asked.

I frowned hard and kept my lips tight. Since when did he give a fuck about me or my well-being? The last conversation we had before I took a few bullets, he told me he was moving his whore onto the same property where our kids laid their heads at night. Lo and behold, both of their stupid asses were standing in my face, which rarely happened. I made it my business to stay on the top floor and out of the way of the fuckery. My life had gone from riches to ratchet in the blink of an eye. I was angry. No, I was more than that. I was vexed as fuck.

"I mean, I don't see why we can't be cordial. We're all adults, right?" Tia chimed in.

I swung my neck around so fast it cracked. "I'm sorry. Did you say something to me?"

She sucked her teeth and turned away to tend to her whining baby, who wasn't willfully taking the bottle she was trying to force into his mouth. The more she tried, the fussier he got until no one could hear themselves think over his screams. *Ugh, worst three months of my fucking life.*

* * *

## Cap

I watched Tia pull out all the tricks she'd learned in her first ninety days as a new mother, but nothing worked. The louder Jr. screamed, the more frustrated she seemed to get.

"Can you please take him, Cap? Nothing I'm doing seems to work," Tia begged.

"Check him for a temperature," Hermès told her.

"What? He doesn't have a temperature. He's fine. He's just fussy!"

"That's not a fussy cry."

"Excuse me? How the fuck would you know what kind of cry *my* son has?"

"Look, I'm not tryna tell you how to be a mother. It's your kid. You do what the fuck you want. I'm just tellin' your stupid ass what I know," Hermès clapped back.

I interjected. "Do it, Tia."

"Do what?"

"Check his temperature."

She sucked his teeth. "Cap?"

"Do you want him to stop crying or not?"

She took the baby back out to his room, and I followed. As soon as we entered his nursery, Tia took his temperature. Her face dropped when she read the thermometer. "He has a fever," she admitted. "what do I do?"

As much as I wanted to tell her step by step what to do to soothe our son, I had no clue. Hermès had always been the hands-on parent while I brought home the bacon and made sure they lived the life they deserved. Instead of responding, I ran back up the path to the main house and found Hermès walking up the stairs toward "our" bedroom.

"Hermès!" I yelled.

She paused and looked down at me. "What?"

"He has a fever. W—what do I do? Call the doctor?"

"What's his exact temperature?"

"Look, can you please come down to see it yourself? Tia is down there freaking out, and I don't know how to calm her and the baby down."

She shrugged. "Sounds like a personal problem to me."

I gritted my teeth. "Please, H. Please..."

She cut her eyes at me before walking down the steps. "Don't ever ask me for shit else after this," she told me.

I followed Hermès as she went to the guest house and into Jr's nursery. Tia rocked him in her arms as he screamed at the top of his tiny lungs. The tears in her eyes told me she was nothing but a petrified new mother.

"What's his temperature?" Hermès asked Tia.

"One hundred point four degrees," she said as her lower jaw trembled.

Hermès outstretched her hands. "May I?"

Tia looked at me and reluctantly handed our son to my wife. Hermès took him into the kitchen and walked over to the sink. She began running the water until it was lukewarm. Tia and I both watched her undress him so delicately and check the temperature of the water with her wrist before gently placing his body inside the sink.

"Cap, give me a baby washcloth," she demanded.

I got what she'd asked for and brought it over to her. I stood to her left while she started bathing Jr. from head to toe as if he were a delicate piece of silk. It was the first time he'd quieted down in what seemed like forever.

"That's it, little man. You're okay," Hermès whispered to him.

The way he calmed under her touch had me astonished. She was a natural. They didn't make 'em like her anymore.

"How are you so good at this?" I whispered in her ear.

"You don't remember this happening with Symphony?"

"This happened with Sym?"

"Yeah, she was around this size, and I remember freaking the fuck out."

"Is that when you called me crying while I was in court?"

"Yeah." She nodded. "that was the time."

I ran my hand down the back of my head. "Damn, I do remember that shit. I rushed home and everything. I wasn't shit but a paralegal back then."

"We were both so scared, and then I called my mom, and she told us what to do."

"You handled it too, way better than I did," I admitted.

"I know, Cap."

"Can I hold him now?" I asked.

"You can do whatever you want. He's your son."

I stepped behind her and looped my arms through her waist, snaking my hands over hers. It felt good holding my son with her. It felt right. At that moment, I'd almost forgotten that Tia was standing just a few feet behind me. I turned my head and felt her glare against the side of my face. It was hotter than the sun. She was fuming. To be honest, I didn't give a fuck. What Hermès had done solidified that we had something that Tia and I didn't: one hell of a history. Hermès was my first love, and I'd lost sight of that along the way. The only thing left to do was work on getting her heart back.

* * *

### Tia

I'd loved Julius Capone from the moment I first laid eyes on him. Words couldn't begin to express how embarrassed I felt to be standing in the presence of him and his bitch of a wife while they reminisced on their children while holding *our* son. I hated Hermès with every breath in me. She was a bitch, and Cap would be so much better without her. I couldn't help but feel disappointed the moment Cap told me that the bullets Hermès had sustained hadn't been successful in killing her. The bitch needed to die. If she were dead, it would make my life so much more straightforward.

They continued to pass intimate looks at each other while I stood beside him. He had no shame. How could he break my heart and flirt with that bitch right in front of *me*? When Cap and I began to get close, he shared the issues in his home life with me, and I vowed to be the missing piece in his puzzle. To Hermès, I was nothing but the young, naïve whore who slept with her husband and had a baby with him. *And I'd do it again in a heartbeat.* Shit, the sex was wild from day one. Bending me over the desk and fucking me in between meetings with clients. *Damn.* Now, he had me feeling like I was only buying time until he told me he would stay where he once hated. I'd be damned if me and my son would be tossed onto the street like yesterday's trash.

I stormed out of the kitchen and fled to my bedroom. As much as I wanted to slam the door, I wanted my son to sleep more. His peace was everything to me, but it killed me knowing that Hermès was the one who could provide him that over me. I was his mother! A few minutes later, Cap's knuckles tapped on the open door. I shot my eyes up at him, burning a hole into his forehead.

"You good?"

I sucked my teeth. "Am I good? Are you serious right now?"

"Jr is good and sleeping. That's what's important, right? Ain't that what you wanted?"

"Of course, that's what I wanted for *our* son, but you aren't gon' stand here in my face and act like I didn't just see you with her the way you were. You don't look at me like that. You still look at her like you love her."

"I do love her," he responded as a matter of fact.

I could feel warm tears simmering behind my eyes. A few more seconds, and they would boil over and spill like water over a sharp cliff. "What is all of this to you? What does having me and your son here mean to you? I'm starting to believe it's not because you love us. It's like all of this shit is a game to you!"

"Why you always questioning whether I love you or not? You're here, my kids are here, just like it's supposed to be."

"Your wife is here, too. You know, the one you claim you can't fuckin' stand half the time. But I guess that's only when you're not cackling like little schoolgirls over your fuckin' kid right in front of me! What the fuck was that even about, Cap? How could you disrespect me like that?"

"Disrespect? Tia, what the fuck do you think this is? Hermès is my wife and will continue to be my wife."

I could feel my face heating up. "What the fuck is that supposed to mean?"

"It means what I said it means, Tia."

"Don't fuck with me, Cap. You and I both know you will lose!"

"Trust me, baby girl, out of the two of us, I'm not the one who needs to be concerned with losing shit. You're under my roof, remember? Now, you can be good with that and play your position, or you can leave, but my son stays with me."

My eyebrows shot towards my forehead. "If you think for one second I'm going to let you keep my son while you and that bitch raise him like he's your own and cut me completely out of the picture, you've got another thing coming!"

Being a new mother meant not being able to come and go as I pleased unless I left Jr. with his father. Cap wouldn't allow me to leave him with anyone else, not even my own family. But his ass had another thing coming if he thought he was going to be the primary parent to my son. The silence that followed was all the confirmation I needed. Cap was on some other shit. I could feel the tables turning, and I had to ensure they turned in favor of me and my son by any means necessary.

## CHAPTER 12

## Sparks Will Fly

**Hermès**

Ever since I did what I did for Cap's bastard son, he was on my ass like white on rice. Although the house was 4,000 square feet, it was impossible to avoid him. I even noticed him falling asleep on the couch in the living room more frequently instead of not in the house at all. The more he crowded my space, the more I craved to be miles away from the house and *him*.

"I think we should go to therapy," Cap said in passing.

I quickly turned my neck back in his direction. "What?"

"Seriously, I think we should go to therapy or marriage counseling or something. We should talk to somebody."

"Talk to somebody about what?" I frowned.

"Whatever you want to talk about...whatever will get us back on track."

"On track? We didn't have an argument, Cap. You had a fuckin' baby!" I snapped.

He lowered his head. "I know that, and I'm telling you that I want us to get some professional help to talk out our shit so we can get over this."

"I'll never get over it," I assured him. He got no cut cards for the disrespect.

The sighs and groans slipping past his lips let me know he was getting aggravated. I didn't give a fuck. It was time I stopped being the only one that was uncomfortable in my home life.

"Can you please just think about it? Sleep on it, at least."

I was unsure why I nodded. Going to marriage counseling had never crossed my mind before the words fell off his lips. In my heart of hearts, I knew that I was still too bruised, but on the other hand, maybe talking to a professional would help me sort out my bullshit. If not for us, at least for my mental sanity. After all, I still had two young black girls to raise into functioning grown black women.

After tucking the girls in bed, I returned to my room when my phone started vibrating. My eyes darted down to the screen and instantly widened. Rio was calling. My heart skipped a beat. We hadn't spoken in months. *Why was he calling? What did he want to talk to me about?*

"H—hello?" I answered after clearing my throat.

His baritone voice flowed through the receiver. "I want to see you."

It had been months, and I was still filled with nervous, giddy energy like a stupid ass schoolgirl. I quickly looked over my shoulder for signs of life in the hallway with the phone pressed firmly to my ear. "When?" I mumbled.

"Tonight. Right now."

Butterflies immediately exploded out of my stomach. "T—tonight?"

"Yeah."

"Why tonight? It's such short notice..."

The woman in me immediately raced to my closet and started searching through it while I waited for him to respond.

"It's my birthday, and for the first time, I don't want to spend it alone."

My breath hitched as I started thinking of excuses to make up for why I needed to leave the house. "Okay, I, um—I can be ready in—just give me an hour, and I'll meet you wherever you want..."

"Good, I'll text you the address."

As soon as the call ended, I went into overdrive. I took the quickest shower in history, thanking my lucky stars that I'd recently come from a wax appointment, so my skin was as smooth as a baby's bottom. I slicked down my edges while throwing a few loose curls in my hair and slid on a black lace top, followed by a black pencil skirt that hugged my curves in all the right places. I tossed my favorite pair of Christian Louboutin heels, my makeup bag, and a crisp white blazer into my over-sized purse and tossed an extra-large shirt and sweatpants on top of my ensemble. The second my feet hit the bottom step, I quickly paced over to the front door to grab my keys and tennis shoes.

"Where are you going this late?" Cap asked, stepping into the foyer with a beer in his hand.

"It's my mom...she called. There's something wrong. I'm going to check on her."

"Do you want me to go with you?"

I shook my head. "No. Someone needs to stay here with the girls in case they wake up."

"Tia is here."

I cut my eyes at him. "Don't you ever say something like that to me. She is not to be anywhere near my kids! They still don't know who the fuck she is or what is going on. They haven't seen her in the three months her ass has been here, and if I have it my way, they never will."

"Okay." He nodded. "call me when you get there."

"For what?"

"I just want to make sure you make it okay, that's all. You've barely left the house since your accident..."

He was right, although his tone of concern annoyed my soul. I hadn't driven anywhere since my accident, but I was determined to make it to Rio unscathed. "Yeah, okay. I'll try. Right now, I gotta go."

Before I could reach the door, Cap extended his hand to grab mine. "Again, can you please just think about going to therapy on your drive?"

I looked back at him while sliding my hand out of his. "I have to go."

The second I got in the car, I pulled out my phone and sat it in the center console while applying red lipstick to my colorless lips. When I was done, I entered the address Rio sent me into my GPS and headed out.

\* \* \*

*"You look beautiful,"* Rio's words greeted me as my heels clicked from left to right until I stood half a foot away from him. Seeing him could make even the proudest woman give in to her animalistic nature. I took a deep breath as my eyes drank him in like warm milk at midnight. I could see the tattoo across his collarbone, peeking through the unbuttoned part of his button-up, and instantly clenched my thighs together. He was perfection personified.

One deep breath.

Two agonizingly sluggish bats of my mascara-stretched lashes.

Three rapid heartbeats later, my lips finally parted.

"What made you call after all this time?"

"How long has it been?"

I frowned. "Three months, Rio."

He flashed his deadly smile at me. "You miss a nigga or somethin'?"

I could feel the heat rushing to my cheeks. "I—I..."

"How have you been, Hermès? Have you been healing properly? Are you being taken care of?"

I let out a light breath, thanking him for putting me out of my misery by changing the subject. "Yeah, I'm pretty much all better... you?"

"Never better."

"So, this is where you wanted to go for your birthday?" I asked, glancing at the restaurant entrance.

"Yeah, it's my favorite restaurant. Have you ever eaten here before?"

"No, I haven't."

"Good. I like it when you experience shit you've never done before with me."

I nodded. "Okay."

The moment he reached out and grabbed my hand, my spine shattered. "Relax, you good with me," he whispered.

After stepping inside the restaurant and looking around, I noticed there were no other diners around, only a chef standing behind a private cooking area. "Where is everybody at?"

"Everybody who needs to be here is here. Besides, I don't like being around a lot of people."

"Yet you own a club...and *The Vault*."

"Let me rephrase that. I don't like being around a lot of people in my private time, so I bought out the restaurant just for us."

"How'd you know I'd agree to see you?" I quizzed.

Rio shrugged his broad shoulders. "I didn't. I would've eaten with or without you."

His response was cold but fair. After all, it was *his* birthday. I decided to quit asking questions and enjoy wherever the night took us. Once seated across from each other, I looked around the candle-lit restaurant while trying to contain my excitement. I'd been to many nice restaurants but had never been romanced, treasured, or simply *seen*. Without his knowledge, Rio was filling gaps in my heart that I didn't know needed to be filled.

After placing my dinner order and letting a swig of chilled wine settle into the pits of my stomach, I felt confident enough to make full-on eye contact with Rio up close. To my surprise, he was staring right back at me.

"It's impolite to stare," I reminded him.

He chuckled. "You think I give a fuck about what's polite and what's not? I'd be a fool not to look at you. It's been too long."

"Oh, so you missed me?"

"Every day," he admitted.

I swallowed hard, not expecting to hear such honesty. Before I melted into a puddle underneath the table, I decided that it would be in my best interest to change the subject. "I have one question that's been bugging me for a while now."

"What is it?"

"The flowers you sent to the hospital...how'd you know where to find me?"

"I keep close tabs on the people I..."

"The people, you what?"

"The people I care about."

"Hmm, so you do care about me?"

"I think you know better than to question me on that."

"I know. It's just nice to hear you say it. You're always so...serious all the time."

"That's just me. Whatever you ask me, I'm gon' be honest and tell you what it is."

"Tell me something I don't know about you."

"There's a lot you don't know about me, be more specific."

"Fine, favorite color," I said.

"Are we really doin' this favorite color, favorite food shit like we're sixteen?"

I sighed. He was right. It'd been a lifetime since I'd even entertained the idea of getting to know another man outside of Cap. Just when I thought I knew everything about the man I married, he showed me I didn't know shit. "It's been a while since..."

"You don't have to explain shit to me, Hermès. I know what it is."

I nodded and elected to take another swig of my wine as I looked around. Silence overcame us, and I silently cursed myself for being awkward and ruining the vibe.

"What's on your mind right now?" he asked, pulling me out of my self-loathing thoughts.

I let out a puff of air. "I—I don't know. Nothing..."

"Bullshit, you're a woman. There's always something on your mind."

"You remember asking me if I had been healing properly?"

"Yeah."

"Well, physically I'm okay, it's just mentally...I'm in hell."

"Talk to me about it."

"Well, for one, my husband ran off and had a baby with another woman and then moved her and the kid into our home. I've been dealing with this shit from the shooting while trying to raise my kids and shield them from the bullshit swirling around them. Now Cap wants to go to fuckin' therapy or marriage counseling like what he did can be fixed, and I'm just..."

"Drowning," he said, finishing my sentence.

I flashed my eyes up at him and nodded slowly. "Exactly..."

"What do you want, Hermès?"

"To keep my head above water without struggling, to raise my kids without the extra bullshit, to get out from underneath all of the drama..."

Instead of responding, he outstretched his arm across the table and grabbed my hand. "Come here. I want to show you something."

"But we haven't gotten our food yet."

"Do you trust me?" he asked.

That was a loaded question, but I nodded anyway. We both got up from the table hand in hand, and I followed him up a winding staircase onto the restaurant's rooftop lounge. A smile instantly stretched across my face as I looked up at the blanket of stars above us.

"This is beautiful..."

"Crazy how you can see the stars this good in the city, right?"

"Yeah, it's easy to get lost in all this."

Rio slid his hand out of mine and wrapped his strong arms around my waist while standing behind me. The grip of his arms around me let me know that when I was in his presence, I was safe. My back rested against his hard chest as we stood and looked up at the sky in a blissful trance. Without saying it, he'd provided me the solace I yearned for.

I gently turned my neck towards his face and kissed his lips. "Thank you for this..."

"All I did was introduce you to the peace you needed. Ain't no need to thank me for that."

I turned to face him fully and wrapped my arms around his neck. We shared a silent moment, saying nothing with our lips, yet our eyes spoke volumes.

"Can I have all of you tonight?" he whispered.

I paused. My body aside, could I allow my heart to be given away more than once? One look into his pools of brown, and I was immediately filled with slow-burning intrigue. Lust, even. I could feel those animalistic urges resurfacing, and I wasn't going to fight them. I couldn't let fear rule me. His fingers gently grazed my cheek, and I felt myself dissolving inside my clothes. Up until that moment, seeing Rio again, let alone feeling him inside me, had only been a fantasy that played on repeat in the back of my mind for months.

"Yes," I breathed.

* * *

## Rio

No matter how broken she felt, Hermès Aleksandra Capone was a masterpiece to me. It wasn't easy to miss the pain on her face after that fuck nigga broke her heart, but the truth was, I knew that fuckin' with me would only cause her more agony in the long run. As much as I didn't want to ruin the moment, I knew I had to man up and tell Hermès the whole truth about how I *really* knew Cap and the business we still had to handle that kept us intertwined.

Using all the willpower I had in me, I released her body from my grasp and took a few steps back. "Before we go any further, there's some shit I need to tell you."

"Is it something I'm not going to want to hear?"

"I don't give a fuck if you want to hear it or not, you gon' listen. I think you deserve to know exactly how I know your husband."

"I thought you told me you two met at your club. Was that a lie?"

"No, there's just more to the story."

Her eyes widened, then followed by a sigh. "Okay, I'm listening..."

I took a deep breath and looked deep into her eyes. "My cousin introduced the two of us one night."

"For what?"

"In my line of work, it's all about who you know, and he knew someone I needed him to connect me with."

"Who?"

"Names aren't important. Just know that once we had a conversation and agreed on what was in it for all parties involved, he dropped twenty bands and joined the club as a sign of good faith. Until I met you, Cap, myself, and my cousin Carlo had been splitting the bag with no problem, with me getting more out of the cut than the other two because I had the most to lose."

"You said up until me...did something happen?"

"The shooting...outside my club. I told you those bullets were meant for me."

"Are you telling me my husband tried to have me killed?" she asked as her bottom lip trembled.

I shook my head. "Greed is a hell of a drug, you know? Your husband and my cousin wanted to cut me out of the picture completely so they could take the twenty-five percent cut they were getting and turn it into fifty between them."

She frowned and folded her arms over her chest. "What exactly is your line of work, Rio? I have kids to think about. I'm not trying to get caught up with you, get sent to jail, and miss out on the next twenty years of their lives..."

I straightened my posture, knowing I already had a response for her. "Then walk away."

"Excuse me?"

"You heard me. Walk away and don't look back for a nigga."

"You don't mean that..."

"If it came past my lips, I meant that shit."

"Rio..." she mumbled, stepping into my chest and wrapping her arms around my waist.

I could feel every bit of anger inside of me unraveling.

*She was my drug.*

*She was my kryptonite.*

*She was simply irresistible.*

All it took was one saddened glance from her glossy eyes up to mine, and I was hers. I couldn't stand to see her cry. My hand swooped underneath her chin, lifting her lips onto mine. The tips of my fingers worked overtime, wiping away her tears as they dripped from her eyes.

"I'm sorry. You're right, I didn't mean that shit."

"Then why'd you say it?"

"You're just as bad for me as I am for you, Hermès. We both know that shit. But as much as I know, I shouldn't fuck with you, here we are."

Looking into her eyes had me unsure if I was heading into heaven or hell, but I no longer gave a fuck. With her was where I wanted to be.

"Let me make it better," I told her.

I gently pressed my lips against hers, securing my hand around her nape. It didn't take long for her to open up to me. I lifted her body into my arms and pressed her back against the nearest wall. My hands snaked all over her body while never breaking the kiss. She moaned in my mouth, and my dick rose to full attention. In one swift motion, I placed her back into a standing position and spun her around. I kissed down the small of her back while lifting her skirt over her ass.

"Mmm," I said, taking a bite out of her ass before burying my face into her pussy from behind.

"Ooooh shit!" she squealed while gripping the back of my head.

My face was instantly drenched with her juices as I reached up and pulled her straps down past her shoulders. After nearly tongue fucking her pussy to climax, I stood up to feast on her hard nipples. She watched me feed for a few seconds before pulling my lips back to hers. Hermès wasted no time pulling my jacket off me, ready to get to the main course. As much as I wanted to be inside her again, I wanted to take my time. She needed to know she was more than a quick fuck. She needed to be fucked like the queen she didn't even realize she was.

We stood in a warm, close embrace, groping as she stepped out of her panties and kicked them to the side. Once again, I lowered myself in front of her and ate her pussy while she stood against the wall. Her back arched like the perfect rainbow after a storm as she threw her head back and lifted her left leg over my shoulder. I French kissed her pussy while sliding my middle and index fingers deep inside her. Her body jerked forward as I flicked my tongue at warped speed. I was putting it all out on the table. If she gave me all of her, I would ensure it was worth her while. I would make my birthday a night neither of us would forget. Hermès was going to be healed from the inside out.

*Every kiss.*
*Every lick.*
*Every stroke.*

I picked her up once more and laid her body flat against the nearest table while unbuckling my dark denim jeans. It was time for the main attraction we'd both been waiting for. I made sure to never lose eye contact with her while sliding deep inside her. She quickly intertwined her legs around my waist, bracing herself for the ride. The pleasure scribed across her face was enough to let me know she was in complete bliss. If that wasn't enough, the digging of her nails into my flesh was my second clue. My thumb circled her clit slowly while I fucked her. She moaned harder.

"Yeah, mmm, shit. Ooooh fuck, yeah!"

"Take this big fuckin' dick, baby girl. I want you to cum all over this fuckin' dick tonight."

"Mmm, shit!" she screamed.

I glided my dick in and out of her sticky, wet slit while smacking my dick against her clit from time to time. With one leg hugging my waist and the other over my shoulder, I slid her Louboutin heel off and began sucking her toes. Her back arched once more, and I could tell she'd never felt so many different ways of pleasure at once. She couldn't control herself.

"Come suck this dick," I demanded.

Hermès sat up with a quickness and climbed off the table. I positioned myself against the edge of the table for balance while she pulled my t-shirt over my head and started kissing down my chest before dropping to her knees.

"Mmm, yeah. Get that shit nice and wet," I told her while pushing her hair to the side so I could get a good view.

*She slurped.*

*She bopped.*

*She gagged.*

A nigga could feel his toes starting to curl in his Timbs. I pulled her back up to her feet and drew her wet mouth onto mine. My body slammed into the nearest chair as she straddled my curve. Wetness engrossed my dick as her voluptuous breasts jiggled in my face. I kept my tongue out to lick whatever came my way. Hermès bounced harder, and I guided her hips to take everything I had to offer her. Every. Single. Inch.

I clenched my teeth. "This dick feel good, baby girl?"

"Soooo fuckin' good!"

I looked into her eyes as I grabbed her by her throat while simultaneously sticking my middle finger inside her tight asshole.

"Ooooh shitttt, Rio! Shiiiiiiiiittttttt!"

Hermès bucked harder against my dick until she climaxed. As soon as I was sure she was done, I lifted her and bent her over the table to beat down her walls from behind.

"Yessss!" she panted while reaching back to spread her cheeks.

"Mmm, you want it deeper, huh?"

I kept my hands planted in her lower back, arching it deeper and deeper. She looked back at me with her mouth in an O-shape.

"Take it, take it, take it," I commanded while wrapping one of her arms behind her back and the other around the back of her neck.

"Fuckkkkkkkk! I'm cumming!"

"Cum! Cum all over this dick!" I told her while tugging at her loose curls.

Even after she came, Hermès continued to throw it back against me. I leaned in and whispered into her ear. "I'm gon' give you my fuckin' seed tonight. Just say the word."

"Yessss!" she cried while digging her nails into my skin.

## CHAPTER 13

# Rock, Paper, Scissors

**Cap**

"I don't like being so far away, Cap! When you told me I'd be staying here, I thought we'd be in the main house, not the guest house like some rejects..."

Tia was bitching, again. The bigger my son got, the more she found something to complain about. I wasn't feeling that shit one bit. As much as I enjoyed watching my son grow big and strong, I spent more time inside the house than with her. Honestly, I was trying to get back in my wife's good graces. I'd decided that I was going to put my best foot forward and do my best to repair our marriage. The problem was, I hadn't told Tia. A part of me never planned to.

"You told me we were going to be together as a family, that me and the baby moving here meant it was you and me!"

Luckily, my hefty investment into my well-being paid off, and I could breathe more easily. Things had settled down, and although some of me still expected some heat, there wasn't any from Rio or anyone else. I still planned to have him killed the moment I moved my family and me the hell out of the state, but until then, I was fine with the hired hittas keeping him at bay.

"Helllloooooo, Cap, do you even hear me?"

I sighed. "Look around you, Tia. We are together, and we are a family. It's not a traditional family, but that's okay, too."

"I expected more!"

"Look, do you believe me when I say I got you?" I asked while placing both hands on her shoulders.

She nodded slowly. "I do, but—"

"But nothin'. Haven't I cared for you since you told me you were carrying my seed?"

"Yeah, Cap, but—"

"Then I just need you to trust me."

"I have been, but this is more than I bargained for, Cap. As much as I want to be with you, I can't keep doing this with you having one foot in and one foot out. I want a serious commitment from you."

"A commitment?"

"Yeah, you heard what I said. Keep your promises to me! You told me that once she was healed up and able to take care of your daughters again, you'd tell her you were leaving her. You were supposed to file for divorce so you and I could finally start our lives together with *our* son!"

"Yo, chill out."

"Fuck it! If you're not going to give me you, then at least give me another baby!"

My eyes widened. Jr. wasn't even a year old, and she was talking about giving him another sibling. "What?"

"You heard me. We should try for a girl so our family can be complete."

"I already have two daughters, Tia. You gave me my son. I'm good. I got what I wanted."

"What about what I want?" She asked.

"You want me, don't you? I think you've made that clear."

Tia sighed. "You know I do, Cap."

"I told you loving me meant loving my life as it stands. You have to love both Symphony and Melody—"

"I could if their mother wasn't still in the picture," she admitted.

I cut my dark brown eyes at her, and she quickly tore her cowardly gaze down to the ground. "You have to love Hermès, too. She's still a part of my life. Ain't shit gon' change that."

"I thought you were going to ask her for a divorce. That's what you said!"

I shrugged. "I know what I said. Shit changes."

Tia had an entire fictional world laid out for us when I knew none of it would ever come true. She was probably right about me bitchin' about my wife and telling her I would file for divorce. Ain't no tellin' what I said when I was knee-deep in her pussy. If she had bet the bank on the two of us running off together to start new lives without all my children, she was in for a rude ass awakening.

* * *

**Hermès**

*"I want you to bear my seed, Hermès."*

It had been a week, and I could still hear Rio's voice clearly in my head, as if he was standing right in front of me. As good as it sounded, I knew it was impossible after I'd been shot. The last thing I wanted to do was disappoint him. We'd never talked about children before. *Were they something he truly wanted? Could he be okay raising and learning to love another man's children?* Everything had healed properly except for my pride. Ever since I found out that I may not be able to have any more children, I felt like half of a woman. Now that I knew having a biological child was something Rio wanted, I decided to go back to my gynecologist to get more tests run. With all the baggage I would already be carrying to his doorstep, I didn't want to go to him without being able to provide him with something he truly wanted. He didn't deserve to have to deal with that, too.

. . .

I sat nervously on the exam table's edge while waiting for the doctor to come in and review my results. My right leg shook nervously as my eyes scanned over the different posters covering the room's walls. *Birth control. Prenatal care. Menopause.* That was all a woman was known for. I shook my head just as my ears perked up to the sound of a knock against the door.

"Come in."

"Hermès! How are you?"

I smiled at Dr. Karrington. "I'm okay...I'd be better if I knew what was in that folder," I said, eyeing the manila folder in her right hand.

"Don't worry, we'll get to that."

She sat on the stool and crossed her right leg over her left before sliding her glasses over her eyes. "Well, as you know, I ran some more tests at your request, and I have good news for you."

My eyes lit up. "What is it?"

"It looks like your left fallopian tube repaired itself on its own."

"And that means what?"

"That you may be able to become pregnant again and sustain the pregnancy to full term."

"Oh my God, are you serious?"

"I'm not saying it will be as easy as your first two, but I am saying that getting pregnant is a strong possibility for you again. You and your husband were trying for baby number three at one point. Is that still something you want to pursue?"

The light her previous words had put in my eyes had suddenly been dimmed with the mere mention of Cap. Truth be told, I didn't know what I wanted. Just knowing I still had the opportunity was good enough for me. That way, if Rio successfully shot up my club, *no pun intended*, I knew it wouldn't be in vain.

"Hermès?"

I snapped back into the conversation. "I—I'm sorry. I don't know if another baby is good for us right now. The timing...it's just...you know?"

She nodded. "I do. Well, I just wanted to give you the good news. Just know that when you decide, I'll be here to bring them into the world, just like I did for your other two angels. How are they doing, by the way?"

"Good, they're great. You know, given the accident and everything."

"Of course, of course."

"I've been trying my best to keep things as normal as possible for them."

Dr. Karrington smiled. "That's what good parents do, and that's exactly what you and Cap are. You're *great* parents."

Her emphasis on the word *great* sunk my heart into my stomach. She wasn't wrong. Cap had always been a great father to the girls. There was no denying that. But he was well below average when it came to being a faithful, trustworthy, loving, and devoted husband.

"Well, I better be going," I told her while standing and collecting my things.

"Take care of yourself now, Hermès."

* * *

*"I need good sex and commitment,"* I sang alongside Monica as her voice bellowed through the built-in speakers embedded in the bathroom walls. Steam filled the room as I let the warm water droplets cover my body from head to toe. To my disdain, the bathroom door swept open, letting in the chilled bedroom air. Cap barged through the door and slid open the shower door.

"Babe."

I cut my eyes at him while trying to cover up my body. He didn't deserve to see me naked. No part of me belonged to him anymore. Also, where did he get off referring to me as his *babe*? I rolled my eyes.

He continued, "There's been something I've wanted to talk to you about."

"What?"

"Turn around and look at me."

"What, Cap? I can still hear you with my back turned."

"I think we should try and have our third baby."

My head shot up from underneath the showerhead as if I'd just been awakened from a deep sleep by a blaring alarm. "Excuse me?"

"You heard me. I think it's what we need to do to get us back to being closer."

I shut the shower off, grabbed my towel to wrap it around me, and pushed past him to step out. The nigga was grasping at straws at that point. "Damn, silly me. All this time, I was thinking we were closer than ever up until your pregnant side bitch pulled up in my damn driveway."

He sighed. "Can you just think about it, please?"

"No."

"No? Why not?"

"Because there is absolutely nothing to think about! I don't know what kind of sick, twisted fuckin' world you live in, but you need to snap back into reality. It's not happening. Besides, you already have your third child with someone else. I'm not going to carry your fourth!"

I stormed out of the bathroom with droplets of water dripping behind me. He had some mothafuckin nerve trying me like that. Who the fuck did he think he was? I wasn't there to bend and break on a whim for his entertainment. He was my husband on paper, but that was it. He didn't get to be the one in control of my emotions anymore. Besides, what was the point of being in a marriage if it was lonely or sleeping in a big bed that stayed empty because he'd rather spend all his time in the guest house with his side bitch? I'd been dealing with a miscarriage of the heart for months, and no one seemed to care but me. I had to face the facts. There was nothing left in my marriage for me to hold onto. Cap and I were through.

As soon as my body was dry and I knew Cap had gotten the hell out of my space, I headed straight for my phone to text Rio.

*Me: Can I see you tonight?*

* * *

## Rio

I simply replied to her text with an address and instructed her to meet me in an hour. That would give me enough time to set things up how I wanted. I'd been battling with my heart and mind over her since the night I stepped foot on her doorstep. I'd never had a woman ask anything of me, and if they did, I never entertained the thought of giving them what they wanted. Yet, I was ready and willing to be anything Hermès needed.

*A protector.*

*A friend.*

*A lover.*

A part of me knew she'd never forgive me for the part I played in doing business with her husband. Not only was I jeopardizing my sanity by fuckin' with her, but her heart as well. She'd already been through so much shit. Who was I to drag her through more? As much as I knew I wasn't worthy or suitable for her, I couldn't leave her alone. She deserved to have a nigga who was in her corner for once, and I was going to show her that she made me want to be that.

*Hermès: I'm outside...I think.*

*Me: Come to the door.*

I watched her get out of her vehicle as her heels clicked from left to right like a Clydesdale in Central Park. There was a perplexed yet intrigued look on her face as her eyes took in her surroundings.

"What is this place?" she asked after greeting me with a hug.

"I bet a construction site was the last place you thought you'd be showing up to meet a nigga, right?"

"Exactly, so... what's going on?"

"Come in, and I'll show you. Just watch your step."

I slipped her hand in mine and led her through the unfinished construction site that would soon be my new home.

"I figured it was only right that you saw my place since I've seen yours," I told her.

"All of this is yours?" She asked, marveling at the unfinished space around her.

"All three thousand square feet."

"What are you gonna do with all this space, Rio?"

I shrugged. "I don't know, you tell me."

"What do you mean?"

"I was thinkin' we could raise a family in it."

As soon as the word *family* fell past my lips, I sunk my teeth into the side of my cheek. I didn't know what the fuck I was saying. Being a family man was never on my list of life goals, but she had the kind of pussy that would make a nigga get her pregnant on purpose.

"We? I never knew you were serious about wanting any of that," she said, piercing her eyes into mine.

"Shit, that makes two of us. A lot of shit changed when I met you. For the first time in my life, a nigga looked at you and saw a family."

"Rio..."

"I know what you been through, but I ain't what you're used to. You gotta understand, you ain't fuckin' with no rookie, Hermès. I been about you since I met your ass. I saw you, and something just clicked. Shit ain't been right since."

* * *

**Hermès**

The rawness of his words fed my soul. He'd managed to touch me without physically laying a hand on me. I parted my lips to speak, and the only words that fell out were, "Thank you..."

"For what?"

"For not running when you found out just how insanely fucked up my life was. For holding me down and allowing me to be free at the same time...you don't know how much that means to me."

"Then tell me," he said.

I sighed, trying to shuffle around all of the thoughts in my head to find one that made sense enough to say out loud. "For years, I've worn these invisible chains on me, and I never realized how heavy they were until you showed me otherwise."

"I already told you, I ain't what you're used to. You deserve a nigga that don't mind hurtin' another bitch feelings to protect yours. I know you ain't never had no shit like that, but I'm just trying to show you how shit would be with me..."

"And I want that, I do."

"Then what's stopping you? Just look around, Hermès. I want a life with you. A life I've never had before. A life I never wanted before you. All this shit sounds crazy as hell, but fuck it. I can't go back now."

I'd fallen for someone I had no intention of falling for. His words let me know he felt the same way. It was scary but raw. It was pure but dangerous. It was beautiful. *It was us.* Rio was the type of man I knew I could learn from. I could talk to him. I could connect with him. I no longer cared about getting a new Chanel bag or being whisked away to Paris on a whim. Rio took the time to understand me and help heal my pain. That was something material items or international trips could never do.

"Do you love me, Rio?"

Silence hung between us like low-hanging fruit.

"I've never been in love before."

"What about a relationship? You ever been in one of those or had your heart broken?"

He shook his head without giving me a verbal no.

"Then what makes you want this so bad?" I probed.

"I see the pain he caused you. I've seen that shit a million times. Shit, I've probably been the one to cause that pain more times than not. I never allowed myself to want to feel anything towards anyone until you. This is why this shit is so crazy to me. I'm building a house to secure a future with a woman I don't know if I'll ever have. You got a nigga sounding crazy!"

"It doesn't sound crazy to me at all..."

"Then what does it sound like?" he asked.

"It sounds like love..."

I watched the wrinkles in his forehead slowly decrease as a slight smirk formed on his face. "Then I guess you have your answer."

As much as it wasn't the right time for his cocky response, I found myself smiling back at him anyway.

"Anything else you wanna know about a nigga?" he asked, opening the door for my prying mind to enter.

He was right. I'd never met another man like him before. I wanted to know the science behind his thoughts, all the way down to his deepest, darkest secrets.

"Yeah, let's play a game."

He frowned. "What kind of game?"

"I ask you a question, and you have to answer it honestly, and then you get to ask me one back."

"That just sounds like gettin' to know each other to me."

I rolled my eyes. "Whatever."

"Ask away. I'm an open book for you."

"An open book, huh?"

"That's what I said."

"Hmm...okay, first question. Do you sing in the shower?"

"Do I look like I sing in the shower?" He chuckled.

I laughed. "When you were younger, what did you want to be when you grew up?"

"Alive," he responded.

I lifted my chin and my eyes toward him while slightly cocking my head to the side. "Care to explain?"

"My biggest fear has always been dying before my time. I never pictured myself living past twenty-five, but here I am. I'm still wise enough to know my days are numbered. Oh, and that was two back-to-back questions, by the way."

"Okay, so you ask me two."

"What is your biggest fear?" he asked me.

I sighed. "Failing my kids. I keep trying to tell myself that I'm doing right by them. I don't want them to be scarred by anything between their father and me. They are the reason I live and breathe, you know? My goal is always to protect them. Not being able to do that scares the shit out of me."

"You are doing right by them," he assured me.

I gave him a half smile while quickly flicking away a premature tear from the corner of my eye. "Thanks..."

"You wanna know some crazy shit?"

"What?"

"I don't know what it feels like to have kids and shit, but listening to you describe how you feel about them is the same way I feel about you."

I stopped to stare at him while repeatedly repeating the question, *'Who sent you?'* in my head.

"What?" he quizzed.

"Nothing...next question."

"Do you see yourself staying in Philly forever?"

"My kids are here...my mom is about thirty minutes away. It's convenient, I guess, but at the same time, you never know where life will take you."

He nodded. "True."

"What about you? Let me guess, hmm...you're a loner, so you'd probably go wherever the wind took you if you felt like it."

"Somewhat, but I got family out here, too."

"Oh yeah? Like parents and siblings?"

"Mom passed from cancer a couple of years back, and I never knew my father. I got two younger sisters, though, and nephews."

"I'm sorry to hear about your mother," I said as I lowered my head out of respect.

"It's fine."

"Are you and your sisters close, at least?"

"Yeah, we are. Both of 'em got pregnant by some ain't shit ass niggas, so I make sure I do what I can to be there for my nephews when I can. At least the oldest one, his pops have been locked up since before he was born."

"What about the younger one?"

"He's too young, but I help my sister out financially when she needs it and try to drop a little knowledge on her ass, but she don't like to listen to nobody."

"I feel like that's how my girls are going to be. The oldest will try to boss the other one around for the rest of her life like a second mom, and she's never going to listen." I chuckled.

"Could you see yourself having more kids?" he asked me.

I gave a half shrug. "You wanna know something funny? Cap and I were supposed to be trying for a boy the third time right before I found out he was having a baby with someone else. So, I honestly just put the idea to the back of my mind. It's not completely off the table, though."

"So I still got a chance to get you pregnant, huh?"

My heart suddenly landed in my throat before I let out a playful chuckle. "How many kids are we talkin', Rio?"

"Shit, however many you're willin' to let me give you."

Although there was a smile on his face, the sincerity in his tone let me know he was far from kidding. Instead of responding, I decided to take the conversation in another direction. "Could you ever see yourself being married?"

"I couldn't see a lot of things for myself before I met you."

Every answer he gave me was straightforward, with no hesitation, as if I'd slipped him a truth serum without his knowledge. It was chillingly refreshing.

"I can tell you've never had a nigga hold an entire conversation with you without tellin' at least one lie," he said, intertwining his long, brown fingers with mine. "Don't worry about it. I'ma fix all that shit. I don't ever want you to be afraid to talk to me about shit, to ask me for shit, nothin'. I want to know you inside and out. That's important to me."

"It's important to me, too."

"Aight then so hit me with some serious shit and stop playin' scared."

"Fine. What's one thing you would change about me if you could?"

"Your confidence."

I stopped abruptly, first looking at the ground, then letting my gaze drift to his face.

"See, right there. Don't shy away from me. Look me into my eyes when I'm tellin' you some real shit. You're perfect to me. I just want you to see you how I see you," he said, bringing his lips to the same breathing space as mine.

"It's your turn to ask a question," I mumbled against his soft lips.

"Is there anything you don't trust about me?"

"No. Will you ever give me a reason why I shouldn't trust you?"

"Never," he assured me before placing his lips against mine.

## CHAPTER 14

# Forever is a Mighty Long Time

**Rio**

*One week later.*

I never thought I'd be standing where I was with no gun strapped to my waist. I was smack in the middle of Hermès living room with a drink in my hand, listening to Cap talk his shit to me.

*"How much will it take for us to be good?"*

I hated a mothafucka who thought throwing money at a situation would instantly make mothafuckas forget. Little did he know, in my eyes, there was no expiration date on disrespect. *'I know it was you, nigga. I have his phone. I should bury you alive.'* I thought to myself. He'd put a hit out on my life, and the only reason I had stayed off his ass for as long as I had was off the strength of my respect for Hermès. I didn't trust that mothafucka one bit. He'd come for my life once, which meant there was nothing he wouldn't do. Instead of responding, I took a sip of my drink.

"So that's why you called me here today? To bribe me, not to kill your ass after what the fuck you tried to do?"

"I realize I fucked up, aight, but this is me trying to right my wrongs and leave the past in the past."

"Puttin' a hit out on my life is not as simple as a right or wrong. I've killed niggas for way less," I schooled him.

It was almost comical that he thought he had the upper hand. If he knew anything, he would know that cats always play with their mice before striking. He needed to watch his back around me.

"Name your price."

"Five million," I said, tossing out a number for shits and giggles.

He nodded slowly as if he was a robot. That number slammed into his head and his bank account even harder. The truth was, I no longer gave a fuck about whether Cap lived to see the sunrise the next day or not, but I still had to be smart. As much as he didn't know it, he possessed something worth more to me than all the money in the world: Hermès.

I told her I wanted her to bear my seed. I'd never said those words to a woman in my entire life, so in my eyes, she was it for me. I'd do whatever to whoever to ensure her safety. Never in a million years did I picture myself as a family man, but she was the first woman to have me thinkin' differently and putting someone who didn't share my blood before myself. I'd fallen for her, hook, line, and sinker.

"That can be arranged," Cap said, snapping me back into the midst of our conversation.

Instead of granting him a response, I nodded. I knew he was just telling me whatever I wanted to hear to buy himself however much time I wanted to give him.

* * *

**Hermès**

I'd taken the girls out to breakfast, followed by Mani and Pedi combos, before bringing them back to the house forty-five minutes before Symphony's birthday party was supposed to start. I was glad I could get around with the girls like I used to. My heart plummeted to my ankles when I stepped inside the foyer. Rio was standing next to Cap with a glass in his hand. He had a little boy standing near his hip that couldn't have been much older than Symphony. *Was this the nephew he told me about? What the fuck was he doing there with Cap? Why the fuck was he a guest at my daughter's birthday party?* Everything inside me wanted to panic. I gripped Melody's hand tighter as Symphony broke free from me and ran into her father's arms.

"There's the birthday girl! Are you ready for your party today?"

"Yes!"

"That's daddy's girl. Now go get ready for your big day!" he said, putting her down and swatting her on the butt.

"Go upstairs, baby. I'll be up to help you get dressed in a second," I told her.

Once both girls were out of earshot, Cap turned to me. "Baby, you remember my client, Rio, right?"

I nodded quicker than I should've. "Y—yeah. It's nice to see you again," I told him.

"It's nice to be seen," he replied smoothly.

Rio had been granted a first-class ticket straight into my bullshit. I could barely stand to look into his eyes, but I knew if I looked away, Cap would notice. "Cap, I didn't know you'd invited an extra guest...and who is this little guy?" I asked, referring to the little boy.

"This is Amare, my nephew."

He looked at me as if to say, '*This is the one I told you about.*' My lips forced a smile, and I nodded. "Will you two be staying for the party?"

Rio's eyes pierced mine as if we were the only two in the room. "If you don't mind."

In a huff, I turned my attention to Cap. "Cap, did Symphony's birthday cake get delivered?"

He nodded back at me. "Yeah, the caterers are already here, and the cake has been delivered."

"How's it look?" I asked.

He shrugged. "It looks good to me."

Without responding further, I trekked into the kitchen, passing by caterers, servers, and party decorators. I popped my head into the fridge, pulled out a half-empty bottle of Moscato, and poured myself an over-sized glass. My heart was palpitating out of my chest so bad I needed something stronger.

"You really gon' drink right before your daughter's birthday party starts?" Cap asked me, walking over to the island where I was standing.

I cut my eyes up at him. "I don't want your bitch anywhere near this party, Cap. I don't want her anywhere near this day. You make sure you keep her locked in that fuckin' guest house if you have to. I don't want to see her fuckin' face," I said, followed by a loud gulp from my glass.

When silence followed that, I snapped my neck at him. "Did you hear what I said, Cap? I don't want to see her fucking face," I reiterated.

He huffed. "Yo, lower your voice. I got you," he said while pulling out his phone.

"Good," I said, tossing the last swig down my throat.

* * *

The doorbell managed to chime loudly enough for me to hear it over a living room full of little girls squealing and laughing. I ushered in more and more of Symphony's schoolmates, cousins, and neighborhood friends. For the most part, she got toys, money, and two of the cutest children's books I'd ever seen, *'Princess for Hire'* and *'Princess Twinkle Toes and the Missing Magic Sneakers'* by Author Kimberley M. I knew both of those would become her new favorite go-to reads when it came to selecting a bedtime story.

"Okay, everyone. It's time to cut the cake," I announced.

Dozens of tiny feet pounded into the kitchen to stand around the large island and sing Happy Birthday to Symphony. Cap picked her up so she could tower over her three-tier princess-themed birthday cake with a sparkling gold crown on the top.

*"Happy birthday to you. Happy birthday to you. Happy birthday, dear Symphony. Happy birthday to you."*

"Make a wish and blow out your candles, baby," I told her.

She leaned in and blew out her candles while holding up her princess crown with her right hand. I slid the knife down the cake and started cutting it into small slices for Symphony and her friends.

"Yo, baby. Cut Tia a piece for me."

I frowned. "Excuse me?"

"Chill, I told her I'd bring her a piece after the party."

"Cut that shit your damn self," I said, tossing the used knife in the sink.

It was unbelievable how quickly Cap could knock me off my square. I'd let his stupidity rain on my parade for the ten thousandth time, and I was sick of it. I grabbed a slice of cake and a pink plastic fork and retired to the corner to watch the girls eat and converse with their friends. I was such a fuckin' loner. As much as I wanted to be the cool mom that all the other moms envied, yet wanted to be just like I couldn't. I didn't make friends. All I gave a fuck about was that my girls loved me. I didn't need friends or anyone's approval but theirs. As soon as I stuffed a forkful of sugary cake in my mouth, I saw Rio approaching me. My back stiffened as heat started to spread throughout my entire body. The sparks between us were big enough to set my entire house ablaze. Every step closer he got, I found myself clenching my thighs tighter and tighter until I could feel my sweet spot throbbing.

"Yo, you good?" he asked.

"Yeah, I'm fine," I said, covering my mouth while I spoke.

"You sure?"

"Yeah...you uh, you enjoyin' yourself?"

"As much as can be expected for a kid's birthday party."

"I didn't know you had a nephew my daughter's age."

"I guess there's still a lot you don't know about me, but lucky for you, you've got a lifetime to figure it out."

My teeth sunk into my bottom lip as I flashed my eyes up at him. It was the first time I'd allowed myself to make eye contact with anything other than the cake in my hand. "That sounds good," I said, flashing him a smile.

It was one thing to have him tell me that he would step in to hang with his nephew, but to see it with my own two eyes did something to me. *So he can take care of another man's child, check.* I noted to myself. "Can I get you something else? Another drink? A piece of cake?"

Rio looked me up and down. "That ain't the cake I'm tryna taste," he growled.

His tone was low, like a murmur, but I heard every word loud and clear, as if he'd said it over the loudspeaker in the middle of Lincoln Financial Field.

"Rio..."

"I'ma chill and get out of your hair. Thank you for the hospitality."

I nodded quickly. "You're welcome..."

He turned to walk away, and I quickly darted to the trash can to toss the uneaten sugary icing I'd scraped off the cake with my fork and made a B-line straight for the half bathroom. I rested my back against the door and leaned my head against it. My heart pounded like I'd just come in from a three-mile run. Rio had entered my space and ruffled me into a dazed ball of emotion. The shit was *not* okay.

Cool water droplets splashed against my flushed skin as I tried to settle my breathing. My heart rate only quickened again when I heard a knock at the door.

"Just a second," I yelled.

I took one last look in the mirror, fixing flyaways in my high bun, and then walked over to unlock the door. To my surprise, Cap was standing there with a frown.

"What?" I asked.

He stepped into the bathroom, causing me to take a few steps back until my calves pressed against the toilet. I watched him shut and lock the door without saying a word. "Tell me the truth, Hermès."

I grimaced. "The truth about what?"

"Are you fuckin' that nigga?"

"Excuse me?"

"Are you givin' another nigga my pussy, Hermès?"

My eyes widened. Cap had never spoken to me like that. It was as if the polish on his educated, well-mannered voice had rubbed off. "Are you crazy? You got the balls to ask me some shit like that when you got your side bitch livin' in my house? Fuck you, Cap!" I yelled, pushing him out of my way.

He quickly turned around and grabbed both of my arms. "I didn't mean to upset you. Come here...it's just...the thought of you bein' with another man...it just makes me crazy."

"That sounds like a personal problem to me," I said while trying to pry myself out of his grasp.

"I said I'm sorry."

I sucked my teeth. "You should be. He was just telling me he was leaving and thanking the lady of the house for my fuckin' hospitality. You're acting like a fuckin' lunatic!"

He gripped my wrists tighter. "I just love you, you hear me?"

"Cap, get off of me."

"Do you hear me?"

"I do, now let go! You're hurting me, Cap!"

"You know what that means, right?" Cap stepped forward until my back was again pressed against the bathroom door. He tossed my wrists around his neck while gripping my waist and leaning down to press his lips against my ear. "You never know what a nigga might do..."

* * *

## Tia

I was standing over Jr's crib, watching him sleep as the reflection of the lights from the main house streamed through his window. I couldn't believe Cap had the audacity to text me and tell me he didn't want me to come to the house for anything until *after* his kid's birthday party. I was fuming on the inside. That message didn't even sound like him. I knew Hermès was behind it.

The second I walked away from his crib, he started to whine and cry. I still didn't know everything about being a mother, but I was learning to listen more before getting annoyed. He was hungry, so I picked him up and walked into the kitchen to fix a bottle.

"Fuck," I mumbled.

There wasn't enough formula for me to make the baby a bottle. I'd asked Cap to pick up some more for me earlier that morning, but still, he hadn't brought it down. He was too busy trying to play the "perfect husband" at his daughter's birthday party. He neglected the needs of his only son.

"Fuck it," I said while rocking Jr in my arms. "we're going to crash that dumb ass party."

All eyes were on me the second I stepped into the house from the patio entrance. Amongst the dozens of little girls running around the house, I locked eyes with Hermès. The look on her face was priceless. I wanted to bottle it up and save it in my memory bank for years. She was disgusted and embarrassed, and I couldn't have been happier. She wasted no time making her way over to me as I started looking around on the countertops for the baby formula.

"What the fuck do you think you're doing?" She asked, squinting her eyes at me.

"Look, Cap was supposed to buy the baby some formula and didn't bring it down. The baby is fussy, and I don't have enough formula for his bottle. The quicker I find it, the quicker you can go back to your *lil party*."

Cap walked over and stood in between us. "Tia...I thought I told you to—"

"Where is the formula you said you'd buy, Cap?"

"Shit, it's in the truck outside. I forgot to bring it in."

"Tell that bitch to go before I make a scene and end this whole shit," Hermès hissed.

He whipped his neck towards her. "Yo, chill..."

"Do you even give a fuck if your son eats or not, Cap?" I asked, loudly spilling the beans to the entire party.

Everything went silent—like driving your car under an overpass in the middle of a rainstorm, silent. The scene Hermès had referred to making had just been made by me, and there was nothing she could do about it. I was tired of me and my son being a big fuckin' secret. I was glad the beans had been spilled. That is until the unexpected happened.

Cap's oldest daughter, a.k.a. the birthday princess, stood in front of the three of us with a puzzled look. "Daddy, is he my brother?"

## CHAPTER 15

# The Heat on High

## Hermès

I flatlined. The eyes of every adult in the room were locked on the four of us and the baby. The next fifteen minutes were filled with dozens of feet putting on shoes and scurrying out of our front door with haste in their step and to go plates of cake in their hands.

*"It was a lovely party!"*

*"Thanks for inviting us!"*

*"I hope she enjoys her gifts!"*

Their smiles were like Band-Aids over a small cut, but that was just the thing about my fucked up ass situation. Band-Aids didn't fix bullet wounds. The second the last guest pulled out of the driveway, Cap closed the door and turned to look at me.

Although he was apologizing with his eyes, he let the words slip past his lips. "I'm sorry..."

"One thing. I asked you for one fucking thing, Cap! I didn't want to see that bitch for one whole day! I wanted one day to fuckin' pretend that that bitch didn't exist! That you breaking my heart was just a bad nightmare! That we weren't where we are right now! And now you bring my child into this bullshit? My baby? You make me fuckin' sick!"

"He—"

"No...no! Fuck you! Fuck you for what you did to me and fuck you for what your mistake did to our little girl today. Her fuckin' birthday! Now I have to find a way to unpack your bullshit to a child, Cap!"

"We can talk to her about it together."

I gritted. "I don't want you anywhere near her."

"She is still my daughter, and we are still a family. Let's go upstairs and talk to her."

My eyes soaked up everything about the worst moment of my life: her stuffed animal collection, bins of dolls and dress-up clothes, and brightly colored comforter set with my daughter's body lying against it. With all the bullshit Cap had put me through, I would've taken even more if it meant that my kids would never have to know about their father's mistake.

*"Baby girl, Mommy, and Daddy have something we need to talk to you about..."*

I fought tears the entire time as I stared at Symphony's bewildered face. My ears burned listening to Cap explain to our daughter that he'd made another baby with another woman who wasn't me.

*"We are all a family...and Daddy loves you all the same," Cap stated.*

I rolled my eyes. *Bullshit.*

My eyes continued to blink all around the room, noticing her keychain collection and the growing library of books in the corner. I couldn't bear to look her in the eyes.

"Do you love Daddy, Mommy?" her tiny voice asked.

*"What?"* My thoughts roared. I wanted so badly to tell her no and that I wasn't behind none of that shit, but I couldn't move my lips. Instead, I looked away while smoothing my hands down the front of my pants.

"C'mon, baby girl. Go get ready for bedtime. We've all had a long day," I told her.

The two of us tucked her in bed and kissed her goodnight. Once I ensured both girls were down for the count, I headed to my bedroom to start unpacking the day from hell I had. As soon as I walked past the top of the stairwell, I saw Cap walking toward me. I cut my eyes at him and continued down the hallway. My fingers wrapped around the knob and slammed the door closed before he could get to me. He opened the door seconds later and stepped in front of me.

"Can we please talk about what just happened?"

"You mean having to tell our six-year-old on her birthday that her father cheated on her mother and had a baby with another woman? I don't think we have shit else to talk about."

He sighed. "You think I wanted it to go down like that? I didn't! But Jr. is just as much my kid as our daughters are, and honestly, I'm glad it's out."

I scoffed. "I bet you are. You get everything you want while the rest of us fight over who gets the biggest piece of you. I can't fuckin' live like this, Cap! I just can't!"

"What are you tryna say?"

"I think we both know what I'm saying. For months, I've gone back and forth over what I wanted and what I could tolerate, and if tonight taught me anything, it was that this shit is too much for me!"

"C'mon, baby. I thought we agreed we were getting through this."

"I know that's what you thought, Cap, but it wasn't until now that I know what I want."

"And what's that? A divorce?"

"Yes, Cap! You can still see the girls whenever you want. You, Tia, and your son can all move out and get your place together, and the girls and I will stay here. We'll figure out the finances, and I'll even go out and get a job if I have to, but I can't do any of this anymore."

My tear-stained eyes flashed up towards his. The pain he felt was apparent. Everything was written all over his face.

"I'll agree to give you your space, Hermès, but if you think I'm letting you go without a fight, you don't know me at all."

I sighed. "I don't want to fight you, Cap. I just want to be free."

"Free to do what? Fuck another nigga?"

I sucked my teeth. "Of course, that's where your mind goes! Free from the feeling of my heart breaking every fuckin' time I see you holding that baby or standing anywhere near that bitch!" I screamed.

It was the first time I'd let it all out in front of him.

"I didn't know you still felt that way..."

"Well, I do. And I know that if I don't get out of whatever is left of this marriage, then I will lose my mind."

"Can you just sleep on it? Whatever you decide in the morning will be what it is. I won't fight you. Can you do that for me, please?"

I blew warm air out of my cheeks and nodded. "Yeah, sure," I said, tossing my hands up.

"Goodnight," he said, walking over and gently kissing my forehead. "just remember what I told you..." he whispered against my skin.

My forehead creased as I shoved him away from me. "You're sick!"

"I'm not giving up on our family. You're *my* wife. You gon' always be that until death do us part," he reminded me.

He stepped back and then turned completely to leave me to myself. The second the door closed, it was as if someone had smacked me into my reality. I had to face the fact that as long as I stayed Mrs. Julius Capone, being with Rio would be nothing more than a fantasy. My heart began to race. I had to think, and I had to think fast.

I searched for my phone, entered the bathroom, and turned on the shower and fan. After a couple of minutes, I sat on the toilet and dialed Rio's number.

"I didn't expect to hear from you so soon," he answered.

"Do you really want to be with me like you say you do?"

"Yes."

"And would you do anything to ensure we could finally be together?" I asked.

"Tell me what you need me to do."

I paused. "I—I want you to kill my husband..."

## Rio

"Say less," I told her after hearing her request. Little did she know, she'd just said the magic words to me.

"Just like that?"

"Just like that," I assured her.

"H—how are you going to do it?"

"The less you know, the better."

She was conflicted about what she'd just asked of me. I knew what was understood didn't have to be explained. In my eyes, she was already mine.

"I just have to make sure my girls are good."

"Don't worry, baby. I got you. I got all three of you."

"Whatever you do, just please be careful, Ro. He's a dangerous man. It's like I don't know who he is anymore, which means I have no idea what he's capable of."

"Ain't a man walkin' this earth that put fear in my heart," I assured her.

"Can you just make sure my kids aren't around when you do whatever you're going to do?"

"Take them to your mother's house in the morning."

"For how long? I need to know how much to pack for them."

"A week."

"O—okay."

"Do you trust me when I say I got every inch of you?"

"Y—yes."

"I need to hear you say that shit."

"I trust you, Rio. You're the only one I do."

I spent the majority of the next day plotting. I couldn't get Hermès' request off my mind. I didn't know what pushed her enough to ask me, but I had my own vendetta against him for trying to kill me. I whipped out my phone to set up a time to meet her for dinner when there was a knock on my office door long before the club had officially opened for the night.

"Come in." I was surprised to see a familiar but uninvited face standing in my open doorway. "what are you doing here?"

"I want to talk."

My forehead wrinkled. "What the fuck do we have to talk about? What? You need money or somethin'?"

"Why you think I always want that?"

"Because that's what you do. Money has been the motive all your life."

"I didn't come for money, Rio. I came to make a deal. I got some information you need."

"I don't need shit," I stated. "what's in it for you, huh? Why you wanna help me all of a sudden? You see what happened the last time you so-called tried to help me out."

"Trust me, this is information you will want to hear..."

## Tia

It had been days, and I was still low-key gloating at how all that shit at the party went down. Knowing that Jr. and I were no longer Cap's dirty little secret felt amazing. He'd kept me waist-deep in my feelings since I moved into his guest house, and I knew things between us all would implode after too long. I'd finally solidified my stake in his life, and unbeknownst to him, I was just getting started. Cap was going to be mine forever. As much as he thought he was in the driver's seat, I was the one calling the shots.

Since the cat was out of the bag about our relationship, it was time to add more fuel to the fire. All I wanted was for Cap, our son, and me to get the hell out of Philly and move as far away from his kids as possible. Whether he wanted more kids or not, I would have our daughter. After she was born, he'd have no need to remember his previous family. To be honest, I didn't give a fuck about his other daughters. As far as I was concerned, they would just be another constant reminder of their mother long after her ass was out of the picture. She was as resilient as a cockroach, and I wanted her time as his wife to come to a close so that Cap could finally focus on the only two people who mattered.

"Ain't that right, Papa," I mumbled to Jr. before nuzzling my cheek against his soft nutmeg skin.

He cooed in my arms before closing his eyes and drifting off into what I knew would be a quick slumber. I put him down in his bassinet as I heard the front door open. Knowing who it was, I neglected to flinch.

"Is he still up?" he asked.

I responded without turning my head to face him, "Just missed him." The room fell silent before I turned around to lock eyes with him. "I see you're still givin' me the silent treatment."

"What the fuck else do you expect from me, Tia?"

I huffed while crossing my arms over my breasts. "I expect you to be a real man about your shit. People know you had a goddamn affair with your paralegal and had a beautiful son. So what? Niggas cheat every day, Cap! I'm sorry you wanted to keep up this façade for your friends, clients, or whoever, but I'm done hiding in the dark. You have a son, all right? Now the world knows it, too."

"They would've known when I was ready to tell them, and my daughter's fuckin' birthday party wasn't the time or the place!"

"What's done is done, right? I don't even know why it matters to you so much anyway. You're divorcing her."

My ears had wholeheartedly expected to hear him agree, but instead, they were ringing from the dead silence that hung in between us once again. Not only did he not respond, but he also didn't even follow up with a simple head nod.

"Cap, you're divorcing her," I told him as more of a command than a question.

"I've been meaning to talk to you about that."

"Talk to me about what? Your divorce?"

"I'm seriously going to try to work things out with her, Tia. I can't have my girls without her..."

"And what about your son, huh? You can't have him without me, so what the fuck you gon' do?" I threatened.

"We'll have to figure it out...as adults."

I scoffed in disbelief. "As adults, huh? Yeah, fuckin' right."

"I know we're all capable of doing it. We just gotta put all the bull-shit to the side and remember to do what's best for the kids."

"And what about what's best for me, Cap? We can have our own family. I already told you I'm ready for another baby. Let me have your daughter, Cap." I said, grazing my hand across his cheek.

It was my sad attempt at winning him back and getting him back in my corner. He gently pushed my hands away and held me by my elbows. "Listen to me, Tia. I love you for having my son. No one can ever take that from you, but my heart... still belongs to my wife. It took me a minute to realize it, but it's the truth."

The way the word *wife* fell off his tongue felt like razor blades to my heartstrings. It was happening. He was breaking up with me for good. I would be a single mother while he lived happily ever after. Julius Capone had me all the way fucked up.

## CHAPTER 16

# For All It's Worth

**Hermès**

*Tick. Tock.*
*Tick. Tock.*
*Tick... Tock.*
*Tick.*
*Tock.*

A ll I could do was watch the clock as I stood inside the therapist's office, waiting for Cap to choose whether to sit on the couch or in one of the other soft-looking chairs. Dr. Zamora's office had a cozy, safe vibe and smelled like fresh linen, which I appreciated. There were fresh, unopened bottles of Dasani water off to the side. My eyes darted to the box of tissues on the coffee table in front of the couch, and I scoffed. *There will be no need for these. I* didn't even want to be there and would ensure everyone knew it. Unfortunately, the appointment had been set before all the shit went down at the birthday party, so I was almost forced to show up. As soon as Cap sat on the left side of the couch, I made my way over to the chair on the opposite side of the therapist and took my seat.

"You don't want to sit by your husband, Mrs. Capone?" Dr. Zamora asked.

"No."

"Very well. Cap told me you were reluctant about coming here today."

"I don't want to be here."

"And why not?"

"What's the point? I know what I want, and so does he."

"And what is it that you want, Mrs. Capone?"

"To be done. To be out and free."

"Do you mind if we unpack that for a few minutes?" she asked.

With my arms folded tightly across my chest, I reluctantly nodded. "Sure."

"Why don't you tell him how you truly feel."

"What if I don't know how I feel?" I asked.

That was a complete lie. I wanted to be with Rio, but I knew the only way we could be together and be happy was if Cap was out of my life for good. The only reason I'd agreed to come to therapy in the first place was so that he wouldn't suspect anything was wrong or different. I sent them away at Rio's request, so Cap and I had no buffer.

"You have to know something, Hermès. Don't think too hard about it. Just try opening your mouth and see what comes out," she told me.

How hard was it to say, *this is it? I'm done. Never again.* For months, I'd tried to push all the bad feelings away, to say I was over all the pain he put me through. The truth was, I was still very much broken. Being with Rio was the only thing that put a spark back inside me.

"You really wanna know how I feel? I feel like the man I vowed my heart and my life to doesn't give a fuck about me, so why should I give a fuck about him? He doesn't love me."

"That's not true," Cap quickly rebutted.

I shook my head. "You don't hurt people you love like that."

"Sometimes the people we love the most hurt us the worst," Dr. Zamora interjected.

I cut my eyes at her and then wiped the back of my hand against my eyes. My vision had instantly become blurred with tears. I'd held all my emotion behind my eyes until I couldn't take it anymore. My hand ripped a tissue from the box. I lied. I *did* need a fuckin' tissue.

"So you're tellin' me that I need to forgive him for not only steppin' out on me, but our family, making a baby with the bitch and then moving the baby and the bitch he fucked into my space, a hundred feet from where my kids lay their heads at night?"

She shook her head. "I'm not saying that at all."

"Good, because I can't do that. I *won't* do that."

"Cap, how does it make you feel to hear that your wife feels this way because of something you did?"

"It fuckin' hurts... We've probably made dozens of mistakes, but we've never come undone like this...not ever."

"Tell your wife how you feel."

Cap turned his attention to me, and I found myself looking into the eyes of the stranger I married. "Hermès, I'm sorry. I'm sorrier than you know. I know what I did was wrong on so many levels, but what's done is done. My son is here now, and I'll never tell you that I regret him, but I will tell you that I regret having him with someone who wasn't you."

I scoffed. "So that's your example of a heartfelt apology, huh? Typical Cap. This isn't a case you're trying to win, Cap! This is our marriage! You have to control everything! The house, the money, the way I loved you. You don't know how to be a husband, and I swear I'm sick and tired of being the only one in this marriage! My kids are the only reason I'm still here! Not us! I don't give a fuck about us anymore!"

"I'm trying to change. I want to be a better husband for her and our kids, but she's not tryna let me do that. You see how hard it was to get her to commit to coming here today. She's still punishing me."

"There's no timeframe on how long it can take someone to heal, Cap. Don't you think her feelings are warranted?"

He nodded. "Yeah, but—"

"There isn't a but. Men have a way of being able to dish things out but can't stand to have their own mistakes thrown back in their faces. Listen to what your wife is telling you. Yes, she's hurt, but with hurt comes pure, unfiltered honesty, and honesty hurts more when you get older."

"And I'm not being punished knowing the reason our marriage is over is living a hundred feet from our fucking home?" I quizzed. "I don't understand how I could give you the world, and it still wasn't fuckin' enough for you! I cooked, I cleaned, I sucked and fucked whenever you wanted. I birthed your children! What more could I give you? You know what, fuck this shit!" I said, standing to my feet.

"Hermès, please, we're finally making a breakthrough here. You want to be heard, right? He's here. He's listening. Let it all out," Dr. Zamora encouraged me.

I snapped my neck back in Cap's direction. I could tell he was simmering with his own emotions from across the room. He needed to hear my war cry. Shit, I needed to hear my war cry. I was sick and tired of being muted, talking without being listened to, being run over and stepped on. There was a thin line between love and hate, and I was about to set the line between Cap and I on mothafuckin fire.

"Do you know how many whispers I heard about you? Silly me to think: No, he loves his family—he wouldn't do that."

"I didn't cheat on you before, Tia. I swear to God. Don't you believe me?"

"Maybe once I would've, but not now. We had a plan, Cap! We were supposed to have our third baby. I thought you were going to be my forever. Do you know how scary it is to start over? You took my happily ever after from me, and now you owe me the opportunity to go find that with someone else *if* that's what I choose to do!"

"So you want to move on with someone else?"

"Are you even listening to me? I'm standing here telling you to your face what the fuck I want—no, what I need from you, and the only thing you hear is that I'm moving on?"

With a defeated look in his eyes, he walked over to me and reached out to grab my hand. "For all it's worth, I'm sorry. I promise you, I'm going to turn all of this around. Please, just say you'll work on forgiving me."

There it was the sad violin shit. I could've even sworn I saw a glimmer of a tear in the corner of his eye. None of his words did anything but add more fuel to the fire raging inside me. "I can't. I don't want to go through this again."

"Baby, please."

I shook my head. "I never broke a single fuckin' promise to you! Not one! You broke your promise to love me forever, so I'm breaking mine. I'm done, Cap. I said it once, and I'll say it again. I want a divorce."

The words fell off my lips easily and were almost too good to be true.

"Cap, are you going to respond to what your wife just told you?" Dr. Zamora asked.

Instead of responding, he cut his eyes at me and brushed past me to walk out of the door, slamming it in his wake. I thought I'd be buried in the ashes of our broken marriage. The therapy session helped me realize that was far from the truth. Being married to Cap had been a fantastic feeling at first. Julius Capone was my beginning, middle, and end until he became a complete stranger. I would never make the same mistake again. After all, the devil never comes at you with horns and a pitchfork.

* * *

## Cap

The fairytale was over. It was clear to me that after the debacle of a therapy session, I needed to place my focus back on Tia and move on with my life since Hermès didn't want shit to do with me. Truthfully, it stung every time I breathed, like a constant reminder that I had bent Hermès until she broke. *A divorce?* I knew I'd toyed around with the idea at one point, but I could never really see myself going through with it.

*"You owe me the opportunity to go find that with someone else if that's what I choose to do!"*

The fury in her voice replayed over and over in my head as I drove back to the house to smooth things over with Tia. I couldn't shake the feeling in my gut that something else was happening. If Hermès thought she was going to move on with the next nigga and have my daughters callin' another nigga 'daddy,' she was seriously mistaken. She was right when she told me that I was controlling. I'd always been that way. Once she realized she wasn't going to get shit in our divorce, she'd be begging me for another chance. If I couldn't have my wife, there was no way in hell I was gon' give another nigga the opportunity. I'd always been the type to want my cake and eat it, too, and up until I moved Tia and Jr. in, I had it.

I pushed those thoughts to the back of my head as soon as I shut the engine off and grabbed my keys to get into the house. Without even removing my shoes, I headed straight to the guest house to talk to Tia and spend some much-needed time with our son. After turning the knob to the door, I walked in through the living room, searching for Tia and the baby. I slowed my pace when I heard her talking on the phone.

*"Yeah, I know...I told you I got you. Shit is all set on this end. Yeah, all right. Bye."*

"Who was that?" I asked, popping around the corner on her ass.

Her eyes widened when she saw me but quickly returned to their normal size. "Cap, you scared me."

"Who was that on the phone?" I repeated.

"Nobody."

My forehead creased. "Nobody? Yeah, all right. You full of shit."

There I was, trying to smooth shit over with her, and she was lying to my face. As much as I wanted to drill her ass until I got the truth out of her, I knew I had bigger shit to talk to her about.

"Jr. is in his room," she told me, changing the subject.

"That's cool. I'll get with him in a second. First, there's something I need to talk to you about."

"Let me guess, you came to reiterate to me how much you love your beloved wife and that you're not leaving her? Because if that's it, save that shit, Cap. I don't even care anymore."

Her nonchalant tone threw me for a loop, but I kept my composure. "That's not what I came to say at all."

"Then what is it because I had planned to put my son down for a nap, pop open a bottle of wine and draw myself a hot, relaxing bubble bath. Oh, and before I forget, I need you to watch Jr. for a couple of hours tomorrow. I've got a job interview."

"A job interview?" I asked.

"Yeah," she said with a blank look on her face.

"I'm putting money away for his future. Trust me, he's going to be good."

"That's great and all, but what about me?"

"The two of you go hand in hand. If he good, you good."

"And where is this *money* located? Who has access to it?"

"Just me for now."

"And you don't think I should have access to his account as his mother? I mean just in case you wake up one day and want to put all our shit out on the curb."

"Won't be no need for all that," I assured her.

"And what would make you think I could trust you after how you've acted so far?" She asked, folding her arms across her chest.

"Do you trust me?"

"You're always asking me that."

"Do you?"

"I—I don't know anymore."

"Do you love me?"

She huffed. "You know I do."

"Then trust me when I say I got both of you. Shit is gonna change real soon around here. All I need you to do is sit tight."

"Do you know how often you've said that to me, Cap? I'm sorry, but I'm going to need more than that. You're always talking so vaguely that I never know what you're actually trying to say."

"Look, Hermès and I are over. I really mean that shit this time. We're going to move forward with the divorce."

Her eyes bulged out of her head before she ran over and threw her arms around my neck. "Do you really mean it, baby?"

"I do. So, listen, I just need you to sit tight a little longer, and once everything is settled with the divorce, I promise you, I'll give you all of the information about the offshore account for our son."

"Baby, listen. I trust that your intentions are good, but divorces don't happen overnight, and they can get nasty. Why wouldn't you move the account and money into my name before signing the divorce papers? That way, she'll have no access to it."

"She can't have access to shit she doesn't know about."

"But what if she does? Or what if she hires a shark ass lawyer to dig into your finances so she can make sure that she's set up for the rest of her life. Her and your daughters. And then where does that leave you, me, and our son?"

I huffed, knowing there was some truth to her statement. I had various offshore accounts that Hermès wasn't privy to. I knew she didn't have a chance in hell of getting access to my money, but I also knew better than to trust a scorned woman. Instead of responding, I pulled my cell out of my pocket and phoned my accountant, Jonathan. As soon as the phone started ringing, I put it on speakerphone.

"Yeah, Cap?" he answered.

"I need you to add Tia's information to the account I had you set up for my son. What information do you need from her to do this quickly?"

"Just a copy of her passport or ID and her email address. I'll send over some forms for her to fill out, and once I receive all of that, I'll make it happen."

"Thanks. I'll text you her email address to get the ball rolling."

"No problem," Jonathan said.

I ended the call just as my eyes landed on Tia's Kool-Aid smile staring back at me. "Thank you, baby," she said, pecking my lips.

Before I could respond, my phone buzzed in my hand. To my surprise, Hermès was calling. Tia caught a glimpse of the caller ID at the same time as I did, and her smile quickly faded into a frown.

"I thought you said the shit was over. You ain't shit but a liar!"

"I'm not lying about shit! I don't know why she's calling me."

"You need to set boundaries with this bitch sooner than later because I'll be damned if once all the divorce shit is over that she is going to be calling your phone any time she wants to. You're spending time with me and your son right now. She needs to respect that shit!"

"She's my wife, Tia. She's not my baby's mother. Plus, she rarely ever calls. Look, I'm not even answering the shit," I said, sending the call straight to voicemail.

She smacked her teeth as hard as she could. "Yeah, whatever. You must think I'm fuckin' stupid, Cap!"

"I never said that."

"You're still fuckin' her, ain't you? Just tell the truth, nigga!"

"Chill with the yellin' and the dramatics, Tia! You just stood here and listened to me call my accountant to give you access to a multi-million dollar account that not even my wife knows about. If that ain't loyalty, I don't know what is!"

Tia huffed. We both knew she sounded like a complete lunatic. "I'm —I'm sorry, okay? I'm not perfect."

"I'm not asking you to be perfect. I'm asking you to be smart," I said, gently kissing her forehead. "let's just agree to put all the bullshit to the side, okay? And you know what?"

"What?"

"To prove to you how over this shit really is between us, I want you to pack you and the baby's things and move into the main house with me. How does that sound?"

She bobbed her head up and down as a smile stretched from ear to ear. "Yes! Yes, that sounds amazing!"

"Good, I'll start helping you move things tomorrow," I told her before going to Jr.'s room to spend time with him.

* * *

A couple of hours later, I found myself back inside the house, knocking on the master bedroom door. When I walked inside, my eyes landed on the two large suitcases Hermès had spread across the California king bed we once shared.

"You called to tell me you're packing your shit?"

"No, that's not why I called."

"Then what did you want to talk about?"

"We need to tell the girls sooner than later, Cap."

"Hermès—"

"No. I'm done with the pretending and all the fake shit. If you don't leave, we will."

"What the fuck do you want from me? You tell me you want a divorce, and now you want to take my fuckin' kids from me all in the same day?"

"This is the bed YOU made, Cap! How many fuckin' times do I

140

need to tell you that? We are here because of YOU! The girls are losing a two-parent household because of YOU!"

My fists clenched, and I could feel myself losing control of the conversation. The room seemed to be getting smaller and smaller as it spun on its axis. I quickly leaned against the nearest piece of furniture that could sustain my body weight.

"When do you want to tell them?" I mumbled.

"I think we need to talk about what we'll say before telling them when they come back from my mother's house. They're getting more curious by the day, so you know they will have questions. And as their parents, we need to be prepared to give them answers. The most important thing for them to know is that none of this is their fault, and none of this has anything to do with them."

I nodded slowly. "Seems like you got it all figured out, huh?"

"What is that supposed to mean?" she questioned.

"You must think I'm a mothafuckin fool."

She frowned. "I have no idea what you're talking about, Cap."

Hermès turned her back to me to walk into the closet and continue packing her things. I walked over to the bed and tossed her clothes out of the suitcase and onto the floor.

"What the fuck is wrong with you?" she yelled.

"You think a nigga don't know when his woman actin' different? Where the fuck did you get all this newfound confidence all of a sudden, huh? You got another nigga in your ear gassin' your shit up, and if you think for one second that I'm gon' let you run off and play house with another nigga and have him raising my daughters, you out your goddamn mind!"

She scoffed. "So I gotta be fuckin' a nigga to see that you're a trash ass husband finally? I think you did a pretty good job of showin' me that shit all on your own."

She was trying to sell me a story I wasn't buying by not acknowledging what the fuck I was saying to her. Instead of feeding into the rage coursing through my veins, I chose a different approach. I was going to let her think I took the bait and let her hang her damn self in the end. I was going to be the one who had the last laugh when all this shit was over.

I unclenched my fist and drew in a deep breath before lowering my voice when I spoke. "All I want to know is if you're sleeping with someone else..."

"And what if I am? How dare you judge me after everything you've done!"

Hermès was visibly pissed. I'd knocked her off her square, and she was having difficulty switching gears. Once again, I was in control.

"I'm sorry if I upset you...I just get so fuckin' crazy over you. If only you could see how much I care...how sorry I truly am for all of this shit."

"Get out!"

"Hermès, I just want to talk this out..."

"I said, get out!" she screamed, pitching her wedding band at me that she'd swiped off the nightstand.

My heels turned toward the door as a smile crept across my face. She'd been caught stewing in her shit just like I was, yet I was the one being portrayed as the *Grinch who Stole Christmas.* The only thing I needed was proof so that I could make sure she only walked away with the clothes on her back when it was time for us to hash out our divorce. *Cap, one. Hermès, zero.*

* * *

It was the small hours of the morning, and I'd woken up with Tia wrapped in my arms. After my ordeal with Hermès, I found solace in the warmth between Tia's thighs. As far as I was concerned, there was no need for me to hide my indiscretions any longer, so once Tia and my son moved into the main house, shit was going to get uncomfortable for Hermès. She made it clear that our marriage was over, so I didn't give a fuck how she felt about how I ran things in *my* house. I slid away from Tia's side and returned to the house for a quick nightcap to put me back to sleep. Just as I was about to get out of bed, I heard the security alarm go off.

Tia jumped up, startled. "What the hell is going on?"

"I think someone is trying to break in," I said, throwing on some pants. "grab my gun from underneath the bed!"

"It's not there. I moved it to be safer for the baby."

I cut my eyes at her and ran straight from the guesthouse towards the kitchen with no way of protecting myself other than my fists. The second I burst through the back door, I was met with the barrel of a gun to the back of my head.

*"Move, and I'll blow your mothafuckin head off."*

As much as I wished I didn't recognize the voice behind me, I knew exactly who it was. Nario Sullivan was standing in my house with a gun pointed at my head.

## CHAPTER 17

# *3:29 a.m.*

### Hermès

Before the sun cracked the sky, I woke up to the sound of the security alarm blaring throughout the house, and my heart immediately began thumping out of my chest. My eyes darted to the bedroom door I'd locked after arguing with Cap earlier that night. I quickly jumped out of bed and crept to the closet to retrieve Cap's gun from the safe.

"thirty-two, two, sixteen," I whispered as my hands trembled.

*CLICK.* The door to the safe popped open, and I slid the gun out without trying to make any noise. Fear clawed through me as I made my way over to the door and placed my hand on the knob. I didn't know where Cap was. All I knew was that I was glad my girls weren't in the house. As soon as I twisted the handle, I heard glass shattering downstairs.

"Fuck," I whispered to myself as I tip-toed closer to the top of the stairs.

The closer I got to the bottom of the steps, I could hear two voices in the kitchen, one being Cap's.

"What the fuck do you want, nigga?"

"I came to collect my five million. From what I've heard, there's plenty more where that came from."

"I told you all I needed was more time, and the money is yours. I'm good at it. You know that!" Cap stressed.

"Then where the fuck is it?"

"Just let me go, and I'll go upstairs and get whatever cash I have on me right now. I have an offshore account, all right? I can have my accountant wire you the rest. You'll be five million dollars richer before the sun goes down tonight. I swear to God!"

"How much you got in the house?"

"I—I don't know!"

"Bullshit!"

"Uh, I—I don't know. Maybe a few hundred thousand! Look, just let me get you the money. The cops are already on their way here!"

With the gun in my hand and my arm extended, I stepped out of the shadows of the living room and into their view. My stomach hit the ground when I saw Cap standing frozen in his step with his hands up and Rio holding a gun to the back of his head. The moment Cap laid eyes on me, his face lit up.

"Shoot him! Shoot him, Hermès!"

"Rio..."

"I said fuckin' shoot this nigga, Hermès! He's trying to kill me!"

I knew what I'd asked of Rio. I knew the reason he had a gun to my husband's head was because I asked him to kill him. Saying it and witnessing it happen were two different things. My entire body was paralyzed in place.

"What the fuck are you standing there for? Shoot this mothafucka!" Cap shouted.

"She ain't gon' do that," Rio said aggressively.

"Why wouldn't she? She's my fuckin' wife, nigga!"

"Then why don't you tell her the truth about who was really behind that drive-by that almost made you a single parent, nigga."

My eyes widened as big as saucers. "W—what?"

"Don't listen to this nigga! Who you gon' believe, baby? Me or him? I'm your husband!"

"And I'm the nigga she's in love with," Rio told him.

His tone was aggressive and oozing so much truth I couldn't dare deny it.

"What the fuck is this nigga talkin' about, Hermès?"

"It's the moment of truth. Go ahead and tell him," Rio coaxed me.

I could see the brokenness behind Cap's eyes as he stared at me, waiting for me to dispel what had just flown out of Rio's mouth. It was the first time I truly believed he could feel how it felt to be betrayed by someone he trusted.

"Well, is it true?" Cap asked.

Before I could respond, there was a knock at the front door, followed by the doorbell ringing. "The cops are here," I whispered.

"Answer the door and send them away," Rio told me. "I'll make sure this nigga keeps quiet."

I looked down at the gun still in my grasp, not wanting to carry it to the door with me but also not wanting to put it down. I placed it on the end table behind a vase and went to unlock the door.

"Hello, ma'am. We received a call from your security company informing us that your security alarm had gone off, and no one was answering the phone to confirm or deny if there was an emergency or not," one officer told me.

"Yes, I'm sorry. My husband accidentally set off the alarm while going to the guest house. Everything is fine."

"Are you sure?" the other officer asked me.

I nodded and tried to force a calm smile across my face. "Yes, I'm sure. We're fine. Thank you for checking on us."

"Okay, well...you and your husband have a good night."

"Thanks, you too!" I said before I closed the door and rested my back against it.

I quickly grabbed the gun and began to put one foot in front of the other until I made my way back into the kitchen. Rio had allowed Cap to sit down while still aiming his gun at him. I knew they were both expecting answers from me. Rio wanted me to finally stand up for myself and tell the truth, while Cap wanted me to put a bullet in the man who had broken into his house and stripped him of his masculinity.

"They're gone," I announced.

"Good," Rio said. "now, go ahead and tell this nigga what's really up between you and me."

"It's true," I confessed. "Rio...Rio and I are in love with each other."

Cap shot me a deadly stare, and I'd never been happier to see a gun pointed in his direction. If it wasn't for that, I was sure he would've killed me.

"Now that that's out, Cap, why don't you tell your wife why you have a gun to your head right now."

"Fuck you," Cap spat.

Rio clenched his jaw before releasing the safety on the gun. Cap's back stiffened, and then he cowardly shook his head. "Fine. We—we had a mutual connection who introduced us. Rio needed a new connect to supply drugs he funnels through his clubs. I had the contact information from someone I represented a few years prior. We all went into business together. After the connect got his cut, Rio, Carlo, and I split the rest of the money three ways. Everything was fine until it wasn't. Carlo wanted more. He convinced me he could do what Rio was doing, and we could make way more money without him, so..."

"So what?" I asked.

"I didn't know you would be at the club, Hermès. I swear to God I didn't know. Those bullets weren't meant for you."

"But they hit me, Cap! The hit you ordered almost took my life away! It almost took me away from my girls! Our girls! How can you even live with yourself?"

"And you're better than me? Sleeping with the fuckin' enemy! He put a hit out on my head, and I told him I'd pay him. That's why he's here! He's here to collect his money. He doesn't give a fuck about you! Congratulations, you played yourself for a fuckin' criminal!"

Cap's words were as cold as ice. I didn't want to believe him. I *couldn't* believe him. Rio wouldn't do that to me. What we had was real, right? My head began to spin as I looked into Rio's emotionless eyes.

"Is it true?" I asked him.

Everything went silent. I realized the reason he was standing in my kitchen was deeper than the request I'd asked of him. Rio had his motives, and I wanted to know the truth.

"What the fuck is going on, Rio?"

## Rio

They say every story has three sides: your side, their side, and the truth. Nine times out of ten, no matter whose story you were hearing, there was always more to the truth than what was being told. I was guilty of that shit. My pride kept me from telling Hermès everything. I thought it would take some weight off me if I told her about the business side of my relationship with Cap. I knew if she knew the entire truth, she would walk out of my life forever, and I couldn't let that happen. I was too invested. She had me wrapped around her finger, and I'd be damned if she'd leave me trapped in my feelings.

"You love me, don't you?" Her voice trembled.

I did. I loved Hermès. Although I couldn't say it flat out when she asked me to my face, I loved her with every breath left in my body. I just knew it no longer made a difference.

"Hermès, I—"

I jerked my neck toward the back door, where another female walked in with panic written across her face. "What the fuck is going on here?"

"What the fuck are you doing in here? None of this concerns you!" Hermès yelled.

"Tia! Tia, go upstairs to my safe and grab all the money you can!" Cap quickly instructed her.

"W—what?"

"You heard what the nigga said. Go upstairs and put the money in this bag," I told her, swiping a black bag off my back and tossing it at her.

"Okay, okay. Baby, what's the code?"

"Thirty-two, two, sixteen."

She darted up the stairs, and Cap diverted his gaze to Hermès. "As soon as this nigga gets his money, I want you and that mothafucka out of my fuckin' house!"

"Fuck you, Cap!" She hissed.

Moments later, she returned downstairs with a filled bag tossed over her shoulder. "Give the nigga the bag so they both can get the fuck out of my house!" Cap yelled.

Tia looked at him and then back at me with a grin. "We good now, Rio. You can go."

"What?" Hermès asked. "how do you even know his name?"

Tia smirked. "Do you want to tell her, or should I?"

"Tell me what?" Hermès yelled.

I drew in a deep breath and let the truth fall off my tongue. "Tia's my sister, Hermès..."

* * *

## Tia

The only thing that would've made that moment better was to have someone there who could capture the look on Hermès' face when she found out the nigga she'd fallen head over heels for was none other than my older brother. The four of us stood at a standoff as the dark truth seeped into the light.

"Tia, what the fuck?" Cap growled.

"How much is in the bag?" Rio asked me.

"About a quarter million dollars," I said, tossing the bag his way. "I'll get the rest to you by tomorrow morning."

Deep down, I knew there was a one-in-a-million chance of Cap leaving his wife to give me the life I wanted with him, so I had to start thinking differently. I was going to get Rio to kill him and then force Hermès to give half of the insurance money to me in return for her never having to see me or my son again.

"Let's go, Hermès," Rio told her.

She stood there with rage coursing through her veins. "Are you crazy? I'm not going anywhere with you!"

"You just gotta trust me. I'll explain everything to you. I swear I will."

"I asked you if I could trust you! I asked you if you'd ever give me a reason not to, and you told me you wouldn't! Knowing you had this shit up your sleeve all along! I don't know who the fuck you are!"

I could barely contain my smile as I watched all the drama unfold right in front of my eyes. Watching Hermès crumble was the icing on a costly cake for me. When I found out that my brother had fallen for her, I knew she'd officially moved on, and there would only be a matter of time before she wanted out. All I had to do was sit tight. Everything changed when she got shot outside of his club. Cap and Rio were a mess over her, and I still couldn't understand why.

"Why don't you just take the money and go? You can buy a new bitch with all the money you're about to come into," I reminded him.

"Shut the fuck up before I put a fuckin' bullet in you!" Hermès yelled at me.

I snickered. "That's funny. That's really fuckin' funny. That pistol in your hand don't make you a real ass bitch. You only a real bitch when you pull the trigger, remember that sweetheart."

"Did you pay him to get in my head?" she asked me.

I shook my head. "Nope, the nigga did that on his own. I had no idea about it for the longest."

"Why wouldn't you just tell me the truth?" She asked Rio.

"Pride is a mothafucka. I swear to God I wish it didn't have to be like this."

"But it does," she said as a tear slid down her cheek.

Rio tossed the bag over his shoulder and walked past Cap and Hermès, who both looked like they were smack in the middle of a nightmare. In the end, they'd both been played. As soon as his hand hit the doorknob, I heard the gun cock. Cap had run over to Hermès and snatched the gun from her hand, aiming it at Rio's back. My eyes bulged with terror. That wasn't a part of the plan.

"Cap, baby! Put the gun down!" I yelled at him.

"If any of you think you're getting out of my house alive, you're sadly mistaken. All of you tried to play me like I'm some bitch! We'll see who has the last fuckin' laugh."

"Cap, baby. Please! Please don't do this. Let him go with the money. It can be you and me just like we planned."

He drew in a frustrated breath while breaking eye contact with Rio's back and turning his attention to me. "You know what, you're right. It's just you and me, right?"

"Yes, of course. It's just you and me. I swear."

"Then prove it," he told me.

"Prove it? How do you want me to prove it?"

He handed me the gun. "Kill him."

My breath stalled. "W—what?"

"You heard what the fuck I said. Shoot that mothafucka! Show me where your loyalty lies, Tia! And you better choose wisely because if you don't, I'll make sure you never lay eyes on our son again."

The tables had turned within seconds. Tears streaked down my face at the mere thought of never being able to see my son again, let alone hold him and watch him grow up. I was a mother first and would do anything to keep him and myself safe. Instead of trying to run, Rio turned to face me. He let the bag on his shoulder drop to the floor, and he spread his arms wide as if he was ready to die. Cap kept talking, but his voice was drowned out by the sound of my ringing heartbeat in my ears. My chest rose and fell with rapid breaths as I closed my eyes and pulled the trigger twice.

*POW.*

*POW.*

## CHAPTER 18

# Out of the Ashes

## Hermès

"You have the right to remain silent..."

Red and blue sirens flashed outside the perimeter of my house as I watched the cops take both my husband and Tia away in handcuffs and shove them into the back of two separate police cars.

"Anything you say can and will be used against you in a court of law..."

My heart spilled out of my chest in the form of tears as I watched them zip Rio's lifeless body up in a body bag.

"You have the right to an attorney. If you cannot afford an attorney, one will be provided for you..."

The last piece of my heart had died with him. Rio's life was taken at the hands of his sister—his flesh and blood. My mind was rattling with all the revelations that had come out in the middle of my kitchen.

*Navy uniforms.*

*Yellow tape.*

*Crimson blood.*

I was sick. Just an hour before, he'd been standing in my presence, defending my honor, claiming me as his. And in the blink of an eye, he was *gone*.

"Hermès, listen to me! Everything is gonna be okay! I'll be out in no time!" Cap yelled before the cop car drove off. "just take care of my kids!"

"I'm getting that divorce!" I screamed.

The moment those four words slipped off my tongue, time stopped. Everyone stared at me in awe. He was sadly mistaken if he thought my tears had anything to do with him or his well-being. As far as I was concerned, they could've thrown him under the jail for the rest of his miserable ass life.

# Epilogue—New Balance

### Hermès

*Six months later.*

I was sick after initially finding out that Rio and Tia were siblings. I struggled between being upset and genuinely disappointed. He'd been living with a closet full of secrets all on his own since the moment he met me and decided to come clean when it was too late for the both of us. Days after the shooting, I found myself replaying every interaction Rio and I ever had in my head, searching for clues. Unbeknownst to me, they were there all along. I just never put the pieces together.

*"Mom passed from cancer a couple of years back, and I never knew my father. I got two younger sisters, though, and nephews."*

*"I'm sorry to hear about your mother,"* I said as I lowered my head out of respect.

*"It's fine."*

*"Are you and your sisters close, at least?"*

*"Yeah, we are. Both of 'em got pregnant by some ain't shit ass niggas, so I make sure I do what I can to be there for my nephews when I can. At least the oldest one, his pops been locked up since before he was born."*

*"What about the younger one?"*

*"He's too young, but I help my sister out financially when she need it and try to drop a little knowledge on her ass, but she don't like to listen to nobody."*

Because Tia had been privy to Cap's illegal dealings than he thought she was, he'd never been released from jail. She flipped on him the second she could, cutting a deal for herself so her son wouldn't end up in the system. Unfortunately for her, she still served time for killing her brother, no matter how much she tried to plead that she'd been brain-washed by the monster that was her son's father. As upset as I was about how things went down between the four of us, I wouldn't let her lie on Rio's name. Besides, after a look through her phone records, it was revealed that a phone call was made to Rio's phone three hours before the break-in. She'd already implicated herself more than she thought.

I took my alimony money and bought a new house in another neighborhood so the girls wouldn't have to change schools. I didn't want their lives to be any more disrupted than they already were, with their father in jail and the man their mother intended to spend the rest of her life with lying six feet under. Cap called weekly, begging me to bring them to visit, but I would be damned if I traumatized my girls like that. All they needed to know was their father was on an extended business trip. It was a trip he'd be on for the next ten to fifteen years with all the charges stacked against him.

Since Melody and Symphony knew they had a little brother, I put my pride aside and allowed for supervised playdates in public places with Tia and Cap's son through Cap's mother. I was glad that young bitch Tia was behind bars for killing her brother, the man that I loved. The worst part about it was her son would have to grow up without both of his parents in his life for a long time. On the other hand, my two girls were great big sisters to their younger sibling, and I knew the same would be true in a few short months when their little brother would be born. I couldn't wait to hold Nario Sullivan, Jr. in my arms. Although I could no longer touch or feel his presence physically, he'd left me with a gift that I'd cherish forever: a son of my own.

"That'll be twelve dollars and sixty-two cents," the cashier told me while handing me a fresh bouquet of red roses.

I reached into my purse and pulled out my card to swipe it.

"Thank you, and have a good day, Miss Baldwin."

I smiled, hearing the sound of my maiden name after so many years. "Thank you. You have a good day, too."

I left the store with my keys in hand and set the bouquet in the passenger seat. I put the car in gear and headed two hours south to the Oak Tree Cemetery, where Rio's body had been laid to rest. There were days that I still couldn't believe he was gone. It was almost as if I'd dreamt him up. Rio was something straight out of my wildest dreams. I liked to think he would've been proud of me for going through with the divorce, taking the girls, and moving out of the house that love no longer lived in. I wasn't strong enough to decide on my own and needed a man like Rio to come into my life and help change my mind. He helped me see my strengths through my flaws.

My ego, morals, or heart had no say regarding Rio. *It never would've worked out between us anyway. I* thought to myself as I held my protruding pregnant belly. When I first laid eyes on Rio, I was a broken woman who never got the chance to know what the warmth of the sun felt like on my face because I'd been hiding in Cap's shadow for six years. Being with him would've required me to change, and I was too comfortable for that. Had it not been for his death, I never would've had the push to be anything other than the miserable wife of Julius Capone.

Being with Rio, if even for the moment, taught me things I would have for a lifetime. There was no way I'd ever be able to teach my girls how to be strong, independent women if I never figured out how to become one myself. Not only did he bring out my inner strength, but he also taught me how to be free. That alone was more than anything money could ever buy.

*"I love you,"* I whispered as I laid the fresh bouquet of red roses across his headstone.

## The End

# *Afterword*

Reader,

Thank you for reading 'Caught Between my Husband and a Hustler.' Please, if you've made it this far, I hope you'll consider taking a minute to tell me what you thought about the book in the form of a five-star **book review or rating**. I thoroughly enjoy reading your reviews and hearing from you as well! Don't hesitate to let me know what you'd like to see from me next! I'm always striving to attract new readers and retain current ones, and reviews are one of the easiest ways to attract readers. If you loved the book, tell a friend, and most importantly let me know!

All my love,
K.L. Hall

*P.S. I created a special playlist just for this series. Check it out by clicking here.*

# About the Author

K.L. Hall is a national bestselling and award-winning author. As a serial storyteller, Hall has penned over three dozen titles in various genres—including African American urban fiction and romance, paranormal, children's books (as Kimberley M.), and non-fiction. Her writing style straddles the intersection of classic Urban and spell-binding Romance.

Highly Acclaimed Series:
 In the Arms of a Savage: (Peaked at #1 in Women's Fiction)
 In the Arms of a Savage 2: (Peaked at #3 in Women's Fiction)
 In the Arms of a Savage 3: (Peaked at #2 in Women's Fiction)

Connect with Me on Social Media:
 Facebook: K.L. Hall https://goo.gl/yGP59B
 X: @authorklhall
 Instagram: @authorklhall and @officialklhall
 Website: www.authorklhall.com

# Also by K.L. Hall

**Novels:**

Diary of a Hood Princess 1-3

Rise of a Street King: The Justice Silva Story *(Spin-Off to the Diary of a Hood Princess series)*

Where He Belongs: A Disrespectful Love Story

Love Me Harder: A Sin City Love Story

Broken Condoms and Promises 1-3

In the Arms of a Savage 1-3

Built for a Savage: Blaze and Camille's Love Story *(Spin-Off to the In the Arms of a Savage Series)*

A Ruthle$$ Love Story 1-3

Fallin' for the Alpha of the Streets 1-2

The Most Savage of Them All: The Wolfe Calloway Story *(Prequel to the In the Arms of a Savage Series)*

When a Gangsta Loves a Good Girl

Caught Between my Husband and a Hustler

**Novellas:**

Bi-Curious: An Erotic Tale

Bi-Curious 2: Tastes Like Candy

A Savage Calloway Christmas *(Christmas novella to the In the Arms of a Savage Series)*

Lovin' the Alpha of the Streets: A Valentine's Day Novella *(Valentine's Day novella to the Fallin' for the Alpha of the Streets Series)*

Awakened: A Paranormal Romance Novella